FOREST OF SILVER AND SECRETS

UNCOMMON WORLD

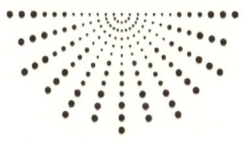

ALISHA KLAPHEKE

To Amelia, Aidan, and Daniel, for all the great ideas

Text copyright © 2018 by Alisha Klapheke
Cover art copyright © 2018 by Merilliza Chan

Library of Congress Cataloging-in-Publication Data
Klapheke, Alisha
Forest of Silver and Secrets/Alisha Klapheke. —First edition.
Summary: Legendary captain Kinneret Raza and a conflicted mercenary join ranks to rise against a vicious forest god that has ruled for one thousand years.
ISBN **(FOR EBOOK VERSION)**
ISBN 978-0-9998314-1-0 **(FOR PRINT VERSION)**
[1. Fantasy. 2. Magic—Fiction.] I. Title.

Printed in the United States of America
10 9 8 7 6 5 4 3 2 1
First Edition

❀ Created with Vellum

1

KINNERET

"**Y**ou're grouchier than normal, Oron." The full-ship rose on a swell, and Kinneret barked at one of her fighting sailors, leaving Oron to continue his determined stewing. "Trim that sail like you've been told twice already," she said to a different sailor. "No, not like that. Move. Let me do it."

Kinneret pulled the lines herself, back straining against her fine new clothing, until the sail was set to match the wind.

"I'm not grouchy." Oron handed her the spyglass and scratched at the mass of tangled braids on his head. "I'm pensive. There is a difference."

"It's not fun. No matter what you call it."

"And that's all I'm here for, Kaptan Kinneret? Your fun?"

"Oh shut up. You know I love you." She dropped a quick kiss on his forehead. He tasted like salt and smelled like the wine she was missing from her quarters. "Despite your thievery."

"My what?"

"And your grouchy pensiveness."

Oron's brow unwrinkled for a heartbeat, and he scanned the horizon, one hand lifted against the sun. "You'll want to take us two knocks southwest before that current up there kicks hard north."

Kinneret hurried to the woman currently in charge of the wheel and passed the information on. Oron could be a fool, but never about sailing. He'd proved that many times over, and Kinneret knew enough to listen to him right away when he offered advice at sea. At sea. Not on land. Especially not on land in taverns.

The coastline was a strip of bare, pale rock in the distance, but the raucous country of Silvania wasn't all that far off.

South of here, her own home of Jakobden—ruled by her friend Amir Ekrem—sat beside Calev's home of Old Farm on the Broken Coast.

Though the waters of the Broken Coast—often called the Pass—held dangerous currents that loved to drag ships into its warm depths, she was well accustomed to them. She knew them, and the city and towns there, like the back of her hand. Yes, Jakobden was a cutthroat port city similar to the place they were headed now. But Jakobden's and Old Farm's ways were second nature to Kinneret. She knew when to steer southward, when to creatively lie to a client—for mutual benefit they didn't understand, of course—when to watch for wraiths.

But Silvania was almost entirely foreign to her.

Wealthy merchants, warring nobility, cursed forests, and sparkling cities of the finest materials combined to create a country no one could help but be curious about. And wary. Of course, being cautious wasn't exactly Kinneret's style.

She had no idea how she was going to help Amir Ekrem

form an alliance between his corner of the Empire—Jakobden —and this foreign land of Silvania. Even if they did share a common enemy—the Invaders had barely lost a siege attack against the Empire's capitol recently. Though Kinneret's soon-to-be-husband Calev might be up to the job, Kinneret was no peace-making delegate. She was far more likely to start a war than develop an ally.

Perhaps that was why Oron was less than happy. Or maybe it was because he had to teach her and Calev Silvanian as well as his native tongue from the Northern Isles for the purpose of rubbing elbows with the foreign traders so they might gain some rare bluehare cloaks and amber beads.

"Let's go over my verbs again."

"Let's not and say we did." Oron produced that stolen bottle of wine, drank, and offered it to her.

"Kind of you to offer me my own wine."

Oron grinned and fluttered his eyelashes.

"That was a gift from Amir Ekrem. For my upcoming wedding."

"And it has been sitting mournfully in your quarters since the day the amir gave it to you."

Kinneret and Calev had yet to set a wedding date. She wasn't putting it off, but life was just so busy right now with all the new and exciting work on the full-ship for Amir Ekrem. Calev wasn't going anywhere. They would marry soon. Just...not yet.

"Can a bottle of wine mourn?" she asked, pushing away from Oron's implication that she was stalling the wedding.

"Oh yes, my dear. Oh yes. I heard its woeful bawling from my humble hammock in this great ship's belly. *I'm all alone, dear Oron. Great master of the drink, please save me from this*

3

wretchedness." He took another swig, then lifted the bottle toward someone behind them.

Calev walked up, wearing a long, emerald green tunic, a blood-red sash, and his jeweled dagger. He waved off Oron's wine offering. Kinneret's spirits rose like she was the ship and Calev was the sea. His eyes flickered over her face and his smile turned sly. A blush filled his cheeks and Kinneret's stomach and neck warmed as she remembered what they'd been doing in her quarters not an hour ago. His lemon and earth scent haunted her skin. Her lips were still sore. She touched them.

Oron groaned. "Please leave off all the gooey eyes. I've never been sick at sea, but you two make quite an effort at ruining my stolid reputation."

As if he ever would be deemed stolid.

Calev ignored Oron and ran a hand down Kinneret's back, over the strip of bare skin between her short shirt and long skirt. His warm fingers danced down her spine, then drifted along the curve of her backside. Sparks of pleasure flashed over her, and she pressed closer, feeling the strength of his thigh against her middle.

Oron lost the fight not to smile at them and stalked away, shaking his head. "Young people."

"We should practice our new languages." Calev's mouth brushed Kinneret's ear and she nearly melted into the decking.

Kinneret tried the *to go* conjugation in both Silvanian and Northern Isle. "I don't think my Silvanian accent is too bad. But the other…"

Calev laughed. "That Northern Isle tongue is a rough one. How they do that *R* sound—I don't think I'll ever get it."

"It's all right. We'll have Oron." She moved to shout to her first mate across the deck. "Why do we need to bother learning the Northern Isle tongue if you're there to speak it, Oron?"

Oron looked up from the compass box, face going dark. "I will not speak it. Not with those people."

Kinneret and Calev both joined him at the box. The wind threw a handful of water into the air and dampened Kinneret's chin and hair. "What do you mean you won't speak it? Of course you will. That's the main reason you're here. Amir Ekrem asked you to help me talk to the Northern Isle folk who will be there for their yearly trade. In addition to trading for bluehare and amber, we might join up with them, as well as the Silvanians. Because I really don't think the Invaders are finished trying to kill everyone."

"I left the Northern Isles for a good reason," Oron said, "and I don't care to spend a single moment in my blessed life breathing the same air as those people ever again."

"Why do you hate them so much?"

"Let's just say there isn't anyone like me—a dwarf—in that upper-caste merchant crew you'll be meeting at Silvania's finest port."

Kinneret and Calev traded a look.

"Yes," Oron said slowly. "I see you have it now. They left me to die on the breakers as a child of ten. Thought I'd never be able to work the land because of my short stature. And they knew I had no magic in my blood to perform greater works around the island." Northern Isle folk had magic stronger than any people, but it faded as they drew away from their islands. "I didn't understand all of that when it happened, but later, I figured it out through stories traded around the sea."

It made no sense. "You're stronger than most of the amir's

handpicked guard. Why would they think you couldn't work as hard as anyone else?"

"Superstition, really. That is what rules the people of the Northern Isles, the people of Snowfallen specifically. It's the largest, most remote of the Isles. And superstition is their weakness. Their crime. If anyone doesn't fit into the all-powerful Fellriki's idea of what Snowfallen should be, then it's the breakers for you."

"Who is Fellriki?" Kinneret asked.

"The strongest *seithr* in their reclusive world." Seeing their looks, he explained further. "A seithr is a person who can carve symbols and make things happen. There is something in the blood up there. Some carry the ability. Others don't."

"Seithr are like…witches?" Kinneret smiled wryly. The slur that was usually aimed at Salt Witches such as herself didn't hold any power over her any more.

"Exactly."

"Snowfallen is the richest of the isles, isn't it?" Calev frowned at the sky as if he could tell what the weather would bring. He definitely couldn't. The poor thing was still terrible at reading the sky's hints. She'd feel worse for him if he weren't so intelligent in other ways.

Oron nodded and wound the end of a sail's tie around a post.

"What is a bluehare anyway?" Kinneret imagined blue bunnies and snorted. Why would that be considered a high-caste sort of thing to wear?

"It's exactly what you think it is. But the animals are very rare and only found on Snowfallen, along with some other very strange creatures. The air on that island…" Oron studied the horizon, a deep line between his thick eyebrows. "The place is stuffed with magic. They'd take over the world if their magic didn't slowly evaporate on long trips."

Kinneret took another look at the compass, then held four fingers above the horizon to measure the sun's height. "Well, we don't have to *like* them, Oron. But we do have to talk to them. It's Amir Ekrem's order, and it's an order that will help us keep our homes safe from Invaders."

"I don't see how people that far north can help, honestly." Calev tilted his handsome head.

She loved how he freely admitted when he didn't understand something. So many believed if they admitted ignorance, they'd be thought of as fools. Calev knew better. Information fed his smarts and Kinneret loved him for that wise humility.

Too bad she was terrible at being humble.

"If the Northerners offer Jakobden a good deal on fine things such as furs and beads," Oron said, "the Invaders may be bribed into leaving us alone. They can take those things from us, then sell them along the Empire's routes for food and water. That is Amir Ekrem's angle. To have items on hand that we can offer to the Invaders if they come by sea to Jakobden."

"It's a long shot," Kinneret said, "but I've heard of things like that happening in Kurakia and beyond."

"Avi has you reading history again, doesn't she?" Calev grinned.

Oron chuckled. "Like trying to teach a cat to enjoy water."

Kinneret's younger sister did have a seriously ridiculous addiction to the amir's library. But it wasn't as if Kinneret didn't read.

"I like books fine, too," she snapped.

"You like them as much as a desert lion would like being shoved into a saddlebag." Calev laughed and Oron joined him.

They were probably right, but they didn't have to be so annoying about it. "Watch yourselves, or this feline might decide to test her claws."

A sailor shouted for attention from the sky cup. "Rough weather ahead."

Sure enough, dark clouds shifted in the distance between the full-ship and Silvania's shore. Several fighting sailors left their posts briefly to pray over the Holy Fire bowl.

Kinneret had thought this trip would be smooth. But with Oron's past and this coming storm, the mission had suddenly grown very, very rough.

Lightning flashed, blinding Kinneret for a moment.

Would her Salt Magic work on the water this far from home?

2

ONA

*Wait. You speak Silvanian. But you're an Invader. And
also, am I dead?*

This was what Ona wished she could say, but
her mouth wasn't currently working. Her lips were nothing
more than sand and dry, little canyons. The rest of her body
wasn't operating either. She moved her eyes—the only parts
that would move—to see that she rode flat, on a wooden cart.
The wheels creaked over the rocky ground. Every once in a
while, a patch of deep, emerald green showed somewhere in the
blurred, watercolor distance. The man closest, the one who'd
spoken to her, the one with the brown and copper hair, glared.
Three other men rode in the cart. They all wore Invader white
and red and a few pieces of metal armor. So yes. She'd been
captured. She wasn't dead. She wished she was. But her heart
was definitely working too. It was doing its level best to beat its
way out of her chest. Not dead. But the battle at Akhayma...

Ona remembered seeing Lucca up on the parapet, his

arrows driving into the enemy, his dark head turning to see her. Then her aunt had appeared in her head like a vision. A memory, yes, but more than that. She had looked at Ona, had told her something. What was it?

Wake, her aunt had said. A hallucination born from blood and pain.

Ona squeezed her eyes shut, not wanting to think about what *Wake* meant, what that vision meant. Ona wasn't Seren. She couldn't see true visions like Akhayma's ruler. Ona wasn't blessed. Nor did she deserve any kind of blessing. Seren had a heart of gold. Ona's heart was most likely a sad shade of gray.

"Yes, that's very good," the Invader who spoke Silvanian whispered. "You look nice and dead again. Keep that up, and maybe we'll both stay alive." The edge of his lips tipped up and he lifted one eyebrow, eyes trained on wherever they were headed.

Acting dead wouldn't be a problem.

Ona's eyes and heart might've been working, but she was as hollow as old bone. Vengeance was the only thing that had kept her going since the massacre at her aunt's villa. And recently, during the battle at Akhayma, Ona had taken down many Invaders like the ones who'd killed her aunt and the one who'd slayed so many in her Silvanian town. But vengeance hadn't satisfied. It'd left Ona empty, shelled, cored.

She had no idea who to be now.

The sky faded from blue to pink, then finally to black, and still the cart bumped along. Pain lay on her body, a constant, burning companion. Consciousness floated in and out of her head as her lungs took air without even asking permission. She wasn't so sure she'd have given it.

"Did Akhayma fall?" she whispered, feeling the Silvanian-speaking Invader beside her.

The man's gaze narrowed under his tawny eyebrows. "No. The Invaders lost. We lost."

Ona almost sat up. Lucca. He could still be alive. He surely thought she was dead. A light flickered inside her chest. Lucca. Her only friend left in the world. He had to hate her. She'd sided with Seren's enemy, his beloved Seren's enemy.

The spark inside Ona's hollow body was made of one thing: the need to ask forgiveness.

Wake.

"Have to get back." Her voice was a croak. "Lucca. Seren."

The warrior's face was suddenly in hers, his gaze staying on the rest of the Invaders, watching them like one does a wasp nest. "What did you say?"

"Back to Akhayma. I need to get back."

The man's eyes flattened like he was somehow disappointed in her words. "Well," he said, "that isn't happening. Now, go back to being dead."

She was trapped. In a broken body. Surrounded by the enemy. Heading to an evil place. But that spark inside burned on, quiet and unrelenting, beating out the one thing she cared about: forgiveness, forgiveness, forgiveness.

3

KINNERET

The pewter clouds swung low and balled like fists as Kinneret turned the stubborn wheel, the wood smooth under her calloused hands. She wished to let the ship go where it may, let the storm have them for a bit to keep damage down, but there was no time for that. They had to be at the main Silvanian port before the most powerful merchants went off for their seasonal hunts along the northern coasts and the Northern Isle folk sailed back into their foreboding region. The Silvanian king would leave for his country estate very soon.

Wind whipped Kinneret's hair around her face. Salty water dripped into her mouth. "Sails down. Tie them up. The wind will take them and we'll be headed under."

Calev and five fighting sailors battled the jib sail's tie. Its end cracked across the deck like a great whip, then circled back. Against the ship's side, it snapped and tripped two sailors who landed hard on the planks. That jib sail needed to come down. Now.

The reedy man in the sky cup climbed down the main mast and hurried to help another sailor knot the lines securing the foresail. Thunder echoed across the unending horizon. A school of fish rippled beneath the waters' surface.

From the stern, Oron gave Kinneret a nod. It was time for Salt Magic. Though the magic never worked as well outside the Pass's cursed waters, it was worth a try.

"Take the wheel, Ridhima."

The woman slid into place, long-fingered hands curling over the indents where Kinneret's had just been.

"Watch it, kaptan!" Calev shouted.

The jib sail's line zipped over Kinneret's head. She ducked. Calev leapt and snagged the tie right out of the air.

Water chilled Kinneret's feet through the spaces in her sandals. The soft, leather bag of salt on her sash was full and ready. She drew out a handful and threw it above her head. The storm snarled like an angry desert lion and swallowed her offering whole.

"Wind and rain,
Strength and pain,
Sea, I hear you,
Sea, I see you.
Sail and dodge,
Push and pull,
Sea, hear me,
Sea, hear me."

The wind sounded different here, storm or no storm. They'd left the Pass now and this stretch of water felt like a stranger, one with a familiar face, but a foreign voice.

A wave reached high and crashed against the jib sail. The ship moaned.

Oron shouted through the open door that led below deck. "All hands! On deck now!"

Sailors streamed onto the deck, some half-dressed with just one boot or missing a shirt.

Oron grabbed the two closest. "Forget tying. Just cut the jib loose. Now!"

They rushed across the deck toward the sail at the bow, pulling knives from their sashes. Everyone else clutched onto posts or the masts. Two sailors lashed down the sealed barrels of Old Farm's finest wheat heads—they'd kept that part of the load above deck to watch for mice. Calev and Oron tied themselves and several others to the main mast.

Raindrops thickened into a deluge. Water drummed onto the decking and soaked Kinneret through. The Salt Magic had to work. She was not about to die from a storm at sea after all she'd been through. No. Even if they were out of the main waters of the Pass and far from where her magic thrived.

Lightning flared from above. A crack sounded, and all heads turned toward the sky cup. A jagged line marred the foresail mast, but the support held. If that mast broke, it would come down on the sailors like a giant hammer and most likely punch a mean hole in the ship. Kinneret gripped a post and clung on, her heart hammering. Shouts and prayers rose from most mouths, from Calev, Oron, and the others tied to the neighboring mast. The sea growled and raised a gray-brown hand to strike again.

Clutching the ship like a friend she'd learned to trust with her life, and keeping her gaze on Calev, Kinneret breathed the wet air in. She closed her eyes, reached into her bag for more salt, and shouted another prayer.

"Sea, be with me,

Hear me, see me..."

The wind ripped the grains from her palm and hissed. It felt like a reluctant agreement.

The ship tilted, then evened out as the rain turned into a drizzle on Kinneret's upturned face. Her shoes grated against the decking and someone called for help.

Opening her eyes, she dared to hope. The clouds broke apart to show the sun. The sea smoothed into rolling hills below. The Salt Magic had worked. But barely.

4

ONA

Ona's eyelids fluttered. Bright, white stars winked back. Her mouth was still so, so dry. The Silvanian-speaking Invader reached toward her ruined vest as the cart ambled on.

"Back!" she tried to shout, but it came out like a rasp of dry air.

The man rolled his eyes, spread the fabric apart, and dabbed Ona's wound with a damp cloth. A shudder rocked her.

"I'm sorry," he whispered. "But I only want you to appear dead, not actually be dead. Don't ask me why. I have no idea."

"Because you miss your native tongue?" she whispered.

His mouth tensed. His hair was a blend of so many colors. She could almost see the hues in bright spots on her old palette. Copper. Sunlight. Mushroom brown. His eyes were gray, but more than that. They had green in them too, bright shots of leaf and moss. Ona told herself to focus. A study in colors was no help in this moment. Or any moment. But she couldn't stop

16

studying the angles of his nose and forehead. No, Ona told herself, knowing lines and shape won't help either.

"Nope," he said, answering her earlier question. "That is *not* it. I'm an Invader. I just speak a lot of languages."

Ona was too tired, too parched, and too hollow to wonder at the lie coloring his words.

He pulled out something green and crushed it. A tangy odor spilled into the air. "This'll keep your wound from putrefying."

Ona's skin caught fire as he pressed the mashed plant into her wound. She bit her lip, a groan pouring out of her.

From the front of the cart, another Invader looked over his hulking shoulder. He barked at Ona's caretaker. The words were sharp and jumbled and they meant nothing to her. All except one word. Dante.

"Is your name Dante?" she whispered.

He speared her with a look, the whites of his eyes bright. "No."

Jabbering back at the man in front, Dante-not-Dante closed Ona's torn vest as best anyone could and hopped off the cart before she could speak to him again in Silvanian.

The men argued. They weren't calling him Dante. It was D'Anton. An Invader name. It just happened to sound a lot like a Silvanian name. Curious.

But why did she care? Even if he was originally Silvanian and named Dante, there were hundreds of Dantes. What did it matter? She knew she'd heard of three or four. Hadn't there been one that worked the docks by the fishmonger's? And another who ran with the street gangs?

Lucca had mentioned the name once. Had said the name like a swear word, like a curse under his breath. Just the once, during a tangle with another group of mercenaries bought by the nasty man who kept a castle by the southern border of Silvania. Why did she remember that so clearly? He'd only done it once.

She wiped her head. Sweat had soaked her hair and face. Fever. From the wound. That's why she was asking herself one thousand questions. Shut it, Onaratta Paints with Blood, she told herself. You're a mercenary, not a lecturer.

But was she a mercenary anymore?

No. The fight was gone from her. She was simply Ona. No one. A husk. A shell.

The dark claimed her blood and bones, and the day faded into nothing.

Rain woke her.

Before the battle that had given Ona this wound, Seren, leader of the Empire, had said the Invaders attacked because of the drought sucking their land dry. Seren had said the Invaders were desperate for food and water. The water droplets cooled Ona's face. This couldn't be the Invaders' land, not with this rain.

And this rain…it wasn't soft or misty like the occasionally damp mornings in the oasis of Akhayma had been. These were tiny, angry drops that smelled like pine.

Ona's eyes flashed open.

Home.

Her heart surged. She fisted her hands.

If they were traveling the edges of Silvania—where she and her only friend Lucca were from—then the Invaders had decided to use a branch of the Great River to get back to their side of the world. The waterways would bring them to the sea, and from there they could slide back into their drought-ridden and desperate homelands. If she ended up there, she was good as dead.

She wasn't sure she cared.

D'Anton had taken over driving the cart while she slept. He tugged the horses' reins gently, and the cart rolled under the spreading, twisting branches of a Silvanian Lob Pine. The angry man that D'Anton had argued with earlier—Ona decided to mentally deem him *Bull*—hopped from the cart, then grabbed a bucket from a hook on the cart's side. Rainwater sloshed from its edges and ran down his thick beard as he drank it down. A third Invader with narrow, icy eyes jerked the bucket from him and gave it to the horses. Bull shouted and punched the man with the really light eyes. Ona would call him Ice King. The man swayed, but held his ground. Ice King lunged, but D'Anton slipped between them, a hand on each of their chests, rain drizzling down his sharp cheekbones and chin. He spoke in quick sentences, his words like shouts too.

Did they have to yell everything?

Ona's head throbbed like someone clenched it in a big, sweating fist. She imagined Invader mornings at home.

Good morning! I need food! The weather is dry today again! Yes! We need to go kill people and take their land! Pass the butter!

Yeah. She'd rather die than spend another second with these people. If she tried to escape, they'd kill her. She had no strength. She couldn't even move most of the time without feeling like she was going to vomit up every last bit of her innards. But that would be fine. She didn't really care to live anyway. Not if she couldn't get back to Lucca and Seren. Her body began to feel oddly light. She was floating. The pulsing in her wound and head pulled her under.

"Get up," D'Anton said, suddenly at her side with one eye watching Bull and the Ice King. He kept his voice low under the splatter of rain on pine needles. "You must stand. Now."

Ona imagined shoving him away, but of course, her arms were dead tree limbs. "I'm dead. Remember?"

"Nope. It's my job to get you tied to this tree for the night. Now help me get you up."

"Just kill me and get it over with. It's fine. Really. You don't even need to feel guilty for killing one of your own. I'm worthless at this point. I'd rather die than be a slave anyway. We're on our way to the river that will lead us back to Invader lands, right?" She swallowed and looked away from D'Anton's pitying eyes.

"You never know where life will take you."

She rolled and, with his hand on her back, maneuvered her fevered body off the cart. The world listed sideways. D'Anton helped her to the ground, and the pine's bed of fallen needles cushioned her as well as any pillow. She leaned against the sap-sticky trunk as D'Anton cut the twine that bound her wrists. He wound a rope around the tree and his tunic slipped over his collarbone.

A brand showed at the spot where his neck met his shoulder. The pink, shiny flesh was just a simple *X*, but it meant he was an Invader and had been through their initiation into manhood. There was something they did that involved fire and fasting, but she didn't know the details. Even if D'Anton had originally been Silvanian, he was forever marked as an Invader. He knotted the tie, and the rope bit her hipbones. Wasn't much of a knot though.

"I could get out of this in a blink if I wasn't two minutes shy of being a corpse."

"I'm sure."

The old Ona would've snarled and told him exactly how she'd be out of that pathetic tie and have his blood on her hands in a heartbeat. That spark inside her, that need to someday see Lucca and Seren, told her to wait, to smolder, to burn quietly until she saw more options than blind violence and pointless snapping.

Ona closed her mouth and watched D'Anton walk away to join the rest of her enemies. The drips of rain and the scent of pines lulled her into a fevered sleep. She almost had the energy to fear what tomorrow might bring, but not quite, not quite.

5

KINNERET

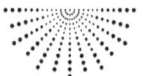

T he main port of Silvania was the stuff of dreams. Tall ships with sails of sunset pink, ruby, sunlight, and midnight blue dotted the bay. Polished skiffs zipped through the crystal water and bobbed beside the ten docks. The center of trade on a worldwide level, Verita saw Northern Isle traders with furs and amber, Kurakian spice merchants, lumber men from the remote Green Mountains, and of course, southern contingents like Kinneret's who brought citrus fruits and specialty grains.

Kinneret, Oron, Calev, and Ridhima left the rest of the sailors in charge of the full-ship. The small group took a smaller vessel into the bay. Kinneret tugged her oar and slid the skiff neatly into a spot beside the second dock. Calev threw their rope over the decorative cleat, which featured two bronze fish facing away from one another, their metal scales green with an aged patina. The port city lay along the lapping water, showing off merchant houses with scalloped columns, paints that cost more than most made in a lifetime, and windows with pointed arches.

"It's too beautiful. My eyes hurt." Kinneret could almost forget she was here on business.

Oron rubbed his hands together, his black mood forgotten in the light of the gorgeous city. "She is a lady in repose, resting near her lover, the sea."

"Poetic."

Calev chuckled. "Can't you appreciate something without relating it to women or wine?"

"Not all of us have the goods in real life." Oron jerked his chin at Kinneret. "*We* poor souls are left with only our imaginations."

They hopped onto the smooth boards of the dock and only a touch of the heat rose up through Kinneret's sandals. Many couldn't afford fine shoes like she now possessed. She promised herself she'd go without once a moon cycle just so she'd never forget that pain.

Her hand strayed to the high-caste silver bells on her sash. A quiet contentedness warmed her as much as the sun because at least *some* of the injustice back in her home of Jakobden had been fixed by Ekrem. They'd helped him into power, into becoming the new amir. It'd been a great victory for the poor of the area because Ekrem actually cared about other human beings, unlike the previous amir.

And now they were here to help Amir Ekrem achieve another success: to gain a strong ally against the Invaders. Though the Invaders hadn't attacked Jakobden, there were rumors about bands of them breaking from the main force that had attacked Akhayma. These bands were said to have been securing boats. If the Invaders ended up with boats, they could possibly move against southern ports like Old Farm's and Jakobden's. Ekrem had told Kinneret, Calev, and Oron that he was willing to provide Silvania food and soldiers if Silvania was attacked. In return, Ekrem suggested the Silvanian king agree to send a number of ships and a military presence toward the Broken Coast to defend Jakobden and Old Farm if Invaders were indeed spotted. It was a good plan. A fair plan. But the king of Silvania was known to be a greedy, cunning man. He wouldn't be easy to deal with and neither would the Northern Isle traders who graced his shores.

When Kinneret, Calev, and Oron were halfway up the dock, another skiff floated up beside them.

Oron stiffened.

The sides of the boat were glacier white and held a party of Northern Isle folk. One woman, about Kinneret's age or maybe a touch younger, stood tall. The wind ruffled her cloak—it was made of the famous bluehare—and tossed the woman's black and silver braids. Her fingers curled around a staff decorated with hundreds of carved runes. Magical *lykill,* they called them. She was a *seithr,* a magic worker from the far north. A blade glimmered at the end of her staff, almost brushing the woman's cheek.

Kinneret put a hand on Oron's shoulder to show him she had his back, but she also faced the party with a smile. They may have come from a terrible culture, but she had business to do with them and she would get it done. All the better if they saw Oron as her high-caste first mate. Success was the best vengeance.

"Greetings," she said in her best Northern Isle tongue.

The woman in the skiff wrinkled her nose.

"Oron," Kinneret said out of the side of her mouth, "greet

them for us and show them you're high ranking despite their prejudices. This doesn't have to go their way, but it does have to move forward. For Ekrem. For Jakobden."

"Fine." Oron shook off Kinneret's hand and opened his arms wide. "Welcome to Verita, northern traders." He said more, but Kinneret couldn't follow the garbled language. She traded a shrug with Calev. Oron might not love this, but at least he was doing his job.

The seithr and an older man with a braided beard joined them on the dock. The man said something fast and sharp back to Oron, who bristled.

Kinneret whispered in Calev's ear. "The man won't look at Oron. See?"

Calev's lip curled.

The seithr did make eye contact with Oron, but she was the only one in the party who would. Kinneret gave her a genuine smile.

Oron held out a bag of silver coins, then faced Kinneret. "How much should I offer for twenty bluehare cloaks?"

Kinneret scrambled for the charcoal and paper inside her sash. She wrote out the number Ekrem's scribe had told them to start with, then handed the information to Oron. He glanced at the slip, then spoke again.

The seithr spoke up for the first time. Oron traded a sentence with her, then she looked to Kinneret and Calev and began to speak in the common tongue, also known as the trade tongue. Kinneret didn't realize any of the Northern Isle folk knew that language.

"Do you think us wrong to push such ones as him from our nests?" The seithr pointed at Oron with her bladed staff. Her words were accented strongly and awkwardly timed, but the meaning was clear. She was asking them their opinion on the Northern Isle custom of killing off children who are different from the average person.

Kinneret knew exactly how she felt about that. "I want to trade with you," she managed to say in the woman's tongue. "But this..." She didn't have the language for this. "It is... disgusting what you do." Some of that was in the trade tongue. Would she understand?

The seithr's eyes flashed. "You do not know us. You do not know our ways."

Calev stepped between the woman and Kinneret. "We want no fight with you," he said in the Northern Isle language.

He took the silver from Oron, who looked about ready to burst into flames. If they didn't make a deal quickly, Oron might just start a battle right here on this dock. Kinneret might end up on a spit for taking that battle and turning it into a war. Her rage colored everything around her.

"Let us trade and be done," Calev said. "This for twenty cloaks. Please deliver them to our skiff here and the woman named Ridhima, who will see it to our full-ship. The skiff is marked with a yellow and black flag." He pointed. "Then you are finished with us and us with you."

Kinneret wanted to shake the seithr. "I don't need to know anything more. This man is my friend, my first mate, the best sailor I've ever met in all my years at sea." She turned to point at Oron, but he was gone.

"Oron! Wait." Kinneret ran toward the city. Oron was already disappearing into the crowd beyond the waterside.

Calev came up beside her, nervous sweat rising on his upper lip. "There. I see him."

Oron wove between two market stalls selling bright orange berries and wooden screens carved from good, Silvanian pine.

Kinneret hurried after him.

Oron's hand went up and he shouted over his shoulder. "I just need to clear my head. Leave me be. I'll meet you tonight. At the king's castle." He disappeared around the pink and white brick corner of a merchant's house.

Kinneret kept on, but Calev stayed her with a hand. "Give him some time. He'll be all right."

"Why does he care what those strangers think? They're a bunch of asses. They are all stuck up in their little islands with that madman Fellriki filling their heads with lies. Who cares what they think?"

Calev's big brown eyes softened. His fingers trailed over Kinneret's elbow and down to the sensitive skin on her wrist. "You know as well as I do that we can't always be sensible when it comes to what we care about." A grin turned his mouth.

A tickling feeling danced through Kinneret's middle and she kissed that grin lightly. "True." Oron was well and truly gone now. They'd never find him in this teeming mass of people and donkeys and carts. "But I'm worried. If he isn't at the king's castle by exactly sundown, I say we go after him."

"Agreed." Calev eyed the dock, squinting against the sun. "Should we go back and try to get the goods Amir Ekrem wanted for the kyros's visit? Or has that ship sailed both metaphorically and literally?"

"I really don't want to talk to those people again. Ekrem can send the kyros something else. One of those old books or some of our silver. It'll be fine."

"True. And Old Farm can offer some goods too. I have no desire to speak with the Northern Isle folk again either."

They started toward the western road, which would lead to the king's castle, and hopefully, a happy ending to this stormy quest. Silvania was a dangerous land full of age-old curses and powerful, rich families battling for land. If Oron landed in the wrong place at the wrong time, he could find himself dealing with new wounds instead of old ones.

6

ONA

"Wake up. We have to go. Now."

Ona opened her sore eyes to see D'Anton's shadowed face. A deep blue like the color of rain clouds covered his cheeks and chin. He whispered, kneeling beside her and fiddling with something behind the tree.

Taller than the two closest pines, the Invaders' fire flickered. Ice King laughed as Bull worked with a whetstone to sharpen his short sword. He splashed a handful of water from a bucket onto the stone and ground the blade with quick, expert strokes.

Pain clenched Ona's wound with corpse-cold fingers. "I think I'm trying to die, so can it wait?"

"You are truly going to meet death if you don't shut your mouth and start running."

"But I'm tied..." She lifted her hands to see the remnants of her bindings. She was free.

D'Anton held a knife by his side, his gaze on the other men. "Come on."

29

He yanked her up. The place where Invader steel had run through Ona's middle roared with agony. It was right below her shoulder and made breathing painful too. She stumbled, but D'Anton pulled her along, over a fallen log that smelled of rot and rain.

"They are drunk on a stash of Silvanian wine they stole from a group of traveling merchants an hour from here. Killed every one of them, down to the young girl with them. Now they've decided you're next. They think it'll be great fun to see how long it'll take you to die either from dicing you up or from a stab wound to the stomach. They haven't decided."

"That's a compliment really," Ona croaked, curious as to why she didn't feel afraid. "They know I'm hard to kill."

"Oh yes. A fine compliment you can take to your grave."

"Why do you care?" She leaned heavily on him as they approached the horse that had earlier been latched to the cart. The horse snorted and stomped the earth.

"I told you that I have no idea why I care about you. But I do. And it's the first time I've cared about anything in a long time."

Ona should've felt warmed, but she felt nothing. Just that nagging need to get back to Lucca and Seren to apologize for all the lies and the treachery.

"I'll mount, then pull you up behind me." Looping the reins over the horse's neck, D'Anton ran a hand down the animal's neck. It snuffled into his shoulder gently. He sprang onto its back with surprising grace, then held a hand down to Ona.

Knowing full well that pain would scream through her with the movement, she gritted her teeth to keep from yelling, grabbed his arm, and swung a leg over. The pain squeezed every bit of energy out of her and she slumped against

D'Anton's back. He tugged her hands forward and lashed them at his stomach so she wouldn't fall off.

Why did she trust this Invader? He could be taking her further into the forest to kill her himself. But he spoke Silvanian. And something about his features, his gestures…well, she was too exhausted and hollow to do much but go along with him.

Bull's voice shot through the trees. He shouted something in their language and crashed toward them.

"Hold on with your legs as best you can." D'Anton kicked his heels into the horse and turned its head east.

Shouts trailed them, and moonlight wove through the pines to touch the ground before the horse's hooves. Rain dripped lightly from the needles and washed Ona's hot cheeks. The sweet water ran into her mouth and around the place where her head met D'Anton's back. His bones and muscles moved under his muddied surcoat. The cloth was rough and chafed her skin, but she couldn't bother to move. The horse jumped, avoiding a rock or something of the sort, and she slid sideways.

D'Anton's hand caught her side. He pushed her back into place as easily as if she weighed nothing. "Stay on, please. Remember, you are tied to me. If you fall, I fall. Then we're both dead and I actually care about dying. I've decided I might have some living left in me yet."

She was about to ask him where they were headed, but the sound of more horses snapped through the wood. D'Anton said something in the Invader tongue and kicked the horse.

Ona turned a fraction to see behind them. Bull and Ice King were a bow shot away. She and D'Anton would never make it riding two on one like this.

"Cut the tie. Let me fall. You go on. We won't win this race."

D'Anton simply shook his head once and kept on. She had to persuade him to leave her. He'd been kind. She was a bad person. He shouldn't die for her.

"They're going to shoot me in the back," she said. "They're already within range."

"It'll be tough considering I broke both their bows before I untied you at the big pine."

"What about axes? Or knives?"

"They don't have any. Just their swords and they won't toss them around. They don't have any money except the little amount they stole from the merchant party. It's not enough for them to get home if they have to buy another weapon."

A gloved hand grabbed Ona's shirt and pulled hard. Her body acted without her mind's direction. Pure muscle memory. She slammed the bottom of her fisted hand into Bull's nose and was rewarded with the glimpse of dark blood running from his nostrils before she collapsed against D'Anton. The move had brought the screaming pain back again and she fought the urge to moan like a beaten donkey. Bull had fallen back, but Ice King kept on, his sword out. He wasn't going to make the same mistake and get within Ona's reach. He'd just nip her spine and see where that took them. Smart.

"He's going to stab me, D'Anton," she said, her voice far too calm.

D'Anton threw something over his shoulder. Their attacker shrieked and both he and his horse tumbled to the forest floor. Ona strained to see what had taken the man down. A blade protruded from the Invader's eye. She shuddered.

She actually shivered at the sight of violence.

Not since the time before the Invaders took her aunt's life at the villa had she been sickened by the death or injury of an enemy.

Who was she?

Onaratta Paints with Blood didn't shy away from gore. She unleashed it and used it to rain down vengeance. But now... now she had no desire at all to spill blood. She didn't even want to see it.

"Is Tantor still following?" D'Anton asked.

She assumed he meant Bull. "Yes. He is behind that copse of beech we just passed. How is someone so drunk so fast?" she mumbled.

"We need cover."

"We need Lucca," Ona whispered, barely audible, half in the world of fevered dreams. The forest blurred and she heard a young voice calling out. "Do you hear that voice?" Now the sound of cracking branches drowned the child's voice. A sigh echoed through the trees and she shivered violently. "Or are they animals? Birds?"

"Birds at night?" D'Anton steered the horse down a ravine, his gaze flitting from their makeshift path to Tantor behind them.

The horse crashed through the brush and into a swathe of land that was bare of trees. Stumps remained along the border, but the rest of the area had been plowed in preparation for planting. A sick feeling slithered through Ona's stomach. The place felt...angry and, maybe...sacred? What an odd sense for a place to have. How could a forest be sacred?

A buzz vibrated under her flesh warning her of something unseen.

Then she remembered something from her childhood. She

ALISHA KLAPHEKE

had passed through an area like this once with her older cousin. They were searching for charcoal to buy. The forest she'd gone through with her cousin had air that weighed on your shoulders and sank into your chest. They hadn't found any charcoal burners' huts there, and they'd fled quickly. This place felt similar to that forest, but this place was…more.

The scent of the pines rose to the point that all other smells were drowned out.

This wood felt somehow…deeper, more powerful. The pull and tug of this specific forest grabbed hold of her like a great hand. She and D'Anton didn't belong here. If she listened hard enough, she could almost hear the felled trees screaming in the spirit world beyond, shouting against those who had cut them down.

Squeezing her eyes shut, she moved her swollen hands inside their ties and tried to relieve some of the discomfort there since she couldn't do anything about the pain of her wound. "No cover here. Let's leave. Go around."

D'Anton's head turned as he quickly surveyed the new border of the forest, a good gallop away. "Doom and donkey balls," he swore in Silvanian.

Ona grinned despite her pain, her hollowness, and the fact that she was probably about to be chopped into pieces. It was a specific curse Lucca had used once when they first tangled with the leader of their chanting crew. "Where did you hear that?" The fever took her words and blurred them into nonsense, and her eyes closed against her will.

When she opened them, she saw a hand reaching out of the dark toward her. The world moved too slowly. Like a nightmare. The hand didn't belong to Bull or D'Anton.

Leaved branches tipped the fingers like brown and green claws.

That strange hand snatched her hair. It pulled hard. Still tied to D'Anton, she fell as he did, dropping from their mount. She was tugged away as D'Anton rolled to his feet and the horse bolted into the night with a frightened whinny. The moonlight showed their attacker. Too long and too slender to be human, he had skin like tree bark and eyes black as pitch. Her body rejected the creature and shook hard. A scream pealed from her burning throat.

D'Anton shouted back, but the words were lost in the rustle of leaves as the tree man dragged her into the line of growth she'd seen beyond the logged strip of land. As far as she could tell, another tree creature had D'Anton.

Panic flooded Ona's veins with energy. She was more herself than she'd been since waking to see D'Anton's face the first time. She took hold of the tree man's hand on her head and planted her feet in the musky-scented earth. With a twist, she had the creature on his knees. He grinned and horror washed over Ona. The look was entirely foreign. Thoroughly evil. Not at all what she cared to see in the dark when she was seriously wounded.

Pain lashed through her wound. Her head swam, tangling her thoughts and knotting up her ability to reason. The tree man stood and grinned again. She nearly vomited with fear. Why couldn't it be bunnies? Or goats? Why did it have to be hellish creatures bent on death and torture and who knew what else?

Before she could move a muscle, two vines wrapped around her ankles. The tree man smiled as the vines jerked her upside down and lifted her into a huge oak. The air in her lungs left in a rush. Black spots floated in front of her eyes. The creature leaned in and wrapped its arms around her and the oak at her back.

With her face smashed against the thing's leg, her heart beat like a hummingbird's in her mouth and in her wound. She lashed out with her hands, trying to grab something she could injure—leg, groin, pressure points—but the tree man didn't seem to feel a thing. A rushing sound filled her ears and the world darkened at the edges. A tingling feeling crawled over her feet, inside her boots. She twisted to look, her body shouting against the movement and her vision blurry.

The creature spoke in soft, unintelligible phrases and the forest seemed to echo him in snaps and the rush of wind through leaves. The tree man moved his head of dark, green leaves and finally Ona could see her feet. Over the rugged boots she'd fought in for years, rough bark grew and spread and covered her to the ankles.

A sheen of sweat covered her back and face.

The creature was somehow melding her with his oak.

A feeling like a giant hand crushing her chest stole what little air she could suck in. She thrashed wildly. "D'Anton," she grunted out. "Bull. Anyone. Help!"

Death would be better than this, whatever this was.

But D'Anton was nowhere around. He was probably going through the same thing.

Still upside down, she strained against her ties as sweat dripped from her neck, to her cheeks, then into her mouth. It tasted like fear. Her nail beds were on fire. Splinters had lodged themselves into her fingers when she'd tried to grab and tear the creature's form. A rotten smell mingled with the pine's scent. The foul stench twisted something wonderful and familiar into a disgusting odor she knew she'd never forget if she managed to escape.

The tree creature's soft refrain needled through her panic and into her ears. Her eyes grew heavy. The pulsing, hot pain in her wound, nails, and head faded. A cool breeze dusted her forehead. The sensation of a man's strong but gentle hand floated down her back and cupped the back of her skull. A sigh left her lips. She knew this was a dream, and that she should properly wake up, but she couldn't help wondering whose hand touched her. A sharp voice in the back of her mind urged her to fight, but she couldn't find the desire. She only wanted the sweet touch, the cool air, the ease of pain.

"Woman. Fight." D'Anton's words slashed through the haze of pleasure and blessed darkness.

Ona opened her eyes to see that her vision was partially blocked by bark. She tried to lift her arms, but they wouldn't move. She was upright now, but she was halfway inside…inside the trunk of the oak. Her throat constricted. She struggled to find her awareness, to blink and breathe and wake up from whatever magic the creature had poured into her.

A light flashed outside the tree. Moonlight on steel. D'Anton slashed a sword through the air and came down on what looked like another tree man. Maybe the same one that had caught Ona. The blade bit into the thing's shoulder and brought it down.

"Can you move? Are you alive?" D'Anton's hair was lank with sweat and looked almost black in the ethereal light of the forest. She was suddenly struck with worry for Lucca. She had to get back to him, to make sure he and Seren were alive and well.

"I'm here." Her throat felt swollen.

D'Anton spun to fight off a second tree creature. The tree man towered over D'Anton. It whipped a long, sinewy arm of ivy, bark, and leaves at D'Anton's newfound sword. But when the thing's branchlike fingers curled around the steel, it hissed and fell back.

D'Anton didn't hesitate. He drove the blade into the thing's chest and ended that one's life.

Ona didn't have time to shudder at the violence now. She was entombed and found she did care about her well-being after all. This wasn't how she wanted to die. If she was going down, it would be in blood and glory, not rot and impotence.

The beautiful male voice whispered inside her head. *Sleep. Feel. All is well.*

"I don't think so." She gathered every shred of will she could find inside her broken body and soul, then drove herself forward. The bark around her cracked.

The first tree man stood, leaving the arm D'Anton had cleaved off on the forest floor, and rushed him. D'Anton shouted, feinted right, and went left. The sword cut the creature in two.

D'Anton hurried toward Ona. "I'll cut you out," he called, his voice now so much stronger than the other one in her mind.

Ona shoved herself forward again and a long piece of wood broke away and fell to D'Anton's feet. The space allowed her arms to move and she braced her palms against the trunk. With one hard push, she blasted through the tree's body and tumbled to the ground. D'Anton caught her arm and helped her up.

Blood rushed away from her head. She shuddered. Pain

returned in waves, pulsing in her ankles, where the tree had laced ivy to lift her, throbbing inside the wound the Invader had given her during the great battle of Akhayma, beating inside her heart, where she ached over Lucca and Seren and all she'd done to hurt them.

D'Anton went down with her and pulled her into his chest. "Is this...all right?"

It was, but she couldn't seem to talk. Who was she right now? She wasn't Onaratta Paints with Blood. Onaratta never would've been caught so easily, given up so soon. But she had to be glad she wasn't that person anymore. That Onaratta had betrayed her dear friends. She'd done the worst and sided with the enemy against the only two people alive who loved her despite all of her flaws.

She spit leaves and dirt from her mouth. "Those things. They're green men, aren't they?" she whispered.

She'd heard about them in childhood stories and legends shared over watered wine and bonfires. Spirits of cursed forests drew humans in and drained them of life. She never paid much attention to the tales, but she did remember something about a god ruling the green men and how this god created these beings from humans with especially strong souls. The more recently created green man, the more powerful. But she didn't recall a single thing about any sword they didn't like or any way to escape them.

"You should run," she said into D'Anton's shirt. He wasn't wearing his Invader surcoat anymore and the fabric against his skin was simple linen. "I am a terrible person and...you should go. Escape while you can. If you can. Use that sword."

He brushed a tentative hand over her back and patted her lightly. "I'm not going anywhere. Besides," he leaned back and tugged his shirt down at the collar to show his Invader brand, "no one will tolerate my presence with this on my flesh. You are the only one who seems to accept that I'm not an enemy."

She laughed—a harsh sound that had nothing to do with good humor. "Because I tend to side with enemies. I told you. I'm terrible."

D'Anton cocked an eyebrow and put two fingers under her chin. His breath was warm on her cheek. "There is nothing terrible about doing your best to protect yourself."

"Even when you fight on the side of wolves who would consume the ones you love most?"

"I'm guessing it wasn't that simple."

"It was betrayal."

"You're allowed to make mistakes. They don't define you."

She set her spinning head on his shoulder and just let this stranger hold her. He was wrong. Mistakes and victories were the very two things that did define a person. But she was too tired to argue.

A branch snapped behind them and Ona's heart jumped inside her chest. They were up in a blink.

"What was that?" D'Anton put a hand on the hilt of the sword he must've found here in the forest's shadowed depths. Markings in the blade caught the few rays of moonlight that filtered through the oaks and pines. Those were no ordinary maker's marks. They were runes like the ones the Northern Isle folk used. Power ebbed and flowed from them like a heartbeat. She could almost feel it bounce against her skin and eyes.

But she was too exhausted to ask about anything. "I need a nap very badly."

Three tree men walked out of the darkness. The largest of them exhaled and somehow it was terrifying.

"No time for a nap now, I'm afraid." D'Anton hoisted Ona up, and then they were running.

Pines tall enough to scratch the stars blurred as Ona raced, zigzagging, through the cursed forest behind D'Anton. She was limping, but the very clear memory of being encased in that oak drove her on like madness. She was numb again, her mind switching off like it often did in a fight. Her boots crunched over the last year's pine needles and crisp oak leaves until an oval of smooth silver appeared in a small clearing.

She and D'Anton both pulled up short.

"I don't like the look of that," he said.

He'd read her mind.

"Go around." Ona began tugging him east, where more trees lurked, thick and dark.

The green men broke into the clearing. Their bark-covered feet—more like roots—pressed the earth where D'Anton and Ona had stood seconds ago.

The creature in the front spoke. The sounds weren't words. They were noises. Branches breaking. Wind in dry leaves. Water over rocks. The whispers started up again.

Shivering, Ona wiped sweat from her brow, then pressed her hands over her ears as they came up to a spot where the growth was so thick, it would be nearly impossible to get through it. She began tearing at the smaller trees and undergrowth all the same. The scent of rot and pine was overwhelming and she was fairly sure she was about to vomit. Not overly helpful during a fight. They had to get through this and out of here.

The tree men slowly advanced, their sounds and the forest's whispers growing louder and tugging at Ona's consciousness.

"It's just water though right?" D'Anton hacked at the growth with his sword, then glanced at the silver pool beside them. The water was too smooth. Too still. "We'll never outrun those things in here." His words were quiet and true.

Ona swallowed a burning lump in her throat and stopped pulling at branches. She did not want to go through the water, but she did like the look of the meadow and thinner trees beyond that silver pool.

The tree men advanced and suddenly sped up, branch arms reaching and mouths whispering, cracking, hissing.

Heart in her mouth, Ona snatched D'Anton and dragged him into the shining surface of the water.

He shouted, but his voice was lost as Ona fell beneath the silver pool's eerie surface.

The water felt like thousands of feathers brushing over her.

The sensation wasn't horrible, but it was definitely creepy. She'd take a blunt hit to the head over this adventure any day. Her mind whirred as her feet paddled to find the surface. The cloudy, metallic liquid surrounded her completely and blinded her of everything else. Her lungs burned with the need for air. There should've been the sound of bubbles or her own yelling—because she was shouting D'Anton's name—but silence shoved into and through her ears.

The silver water leaked through her clamped-shut lips and into her ears and snaked through her hair. A sound like an army of horses rose in her mind.

Then she was run through with a sword.

In the same place she'd already been wounded.

Eyes slamming shut against the fierce pain, she grabbed at the wound. But there was no sword. No new wound. Only the slightly healed one. But it pulsed like a fresh cut. Her head went light and her stomach flipped.

A hand grabbed her back and she struggled against it, her lungs filling. She was dying. This was death, here to claim her inside this magic pool of horror and pain.

The fingers clutching her clothes yanked hard and pulled her free of the silver water.

D'Anton leaned over her as she turned onto her side and vomited.

He put a hand on her back. His eyes were on the forest beyond.

Were the creatures gone? Was she dead?

Ona coughed and sat up, the new pain the pool had brought faded and only the true pain from her healing wound thudded in time with her panicked heart. She touched that wound, making very sure she was right and that she hadn't been somehow run through again under that water.

The silvery stuff dripped from D'Anton's confused face. His eyebrows knitted and his dimpled chin moved under the beginnings of a beard. "Did the water hurt you?"

The forest was quiet. The meadow was free of any tree men. "Are they really gone?"

"Well, I don't see them, so let's be optimistic."

"That pool." The surface was still. No ripples. She shivered and twisted to vomit again. "It's poison. It...I was wounded again. In the same place. I heard the Invaders' horses..."

"You relived your worst moment."

Ona nodded. She felt like a tiny girl again. Small. Lacking muscles or experience or skills. Gritting her teeth, she stood and jerked her chin at the sword D'Anton had obviously dropped on the forest floor.

"Time to tell me where you found that."

"Are swords no longer a favorite of yours?"

43

"Nothing that comes from this place is my favorite."

"I feel the same." He retrieved the weapon, and they began walking back the way they'd come.

She hated it, but there really wasn't any other way out of here. She was not going back through that cursed water.

"I found the sword beside the oak that took you." Tucking the sword into his belt, he frowned. The sky beyond the trees was growing lighter. The morning showed a cut below his ear. Blood had crusted in his hair, and he was limping nearly as much as she was. "Blackened growth surrounded the blade, and well, with all those strange symbols—it had to be powerful in some way. I grabbed the thing and hoped for the best."

"It worked pretty well against the green men. I wonder if that's Northern Isle magic in those symbols."

"I don't know. I didn't think their magic worked outside the isles, but I'm no expert. This may be made from a steel I haven't run into yet."

"Let's not say *sword* and *run into* in the same sentence for while, all right?"

The side of D'Anton's mouth lifted, and Ona wondered what it would be like to kiss him. She swallowed, shocked at the fleeting thought. She'd thought she was too beaten down to think of kissing anyone ever again.

D'Anton turned and walked backward to talk to her. He was surprisingly nimble. "The silver pool didn't injure me, thanks for asking."

Guilt tugged at Ona. Despite all her lessons, she was still thoroughly selfish. "I'm sorry. I'm glad you weren't hurt."

As he turned, his shirt moved down, pulled by the sword he'd tucked into his belt.

Ona's mouth fell open. "Your Invader brand. It's gone."

D'Anton froze, then clutched at his shirt. He craned his neck to try and see, then gave that up and moved his fingers over the formerly burned and scarred spot. The skin there was the same olive tone as the rest of him.

His face changed. His eyes had been haunted and dark. Now the light irises brightened and the lines around his mouth faded. "It is. It's gone."

"You're not an Invader anymore. The silver pool cursed me and blessed you. Typical."

D'Anton rushed toward Ona. She tensed but was too fatigued to react as he grabbed her up gently, hugged her, and planted a kiss on her cheek. He lifted his hands in the air and his feet moved in a quick little dance. "I can't believe it!"

Recognition shocked Ona.

She had seen that dance. When? Where? She shook her head. She was thinking about all the wrong things. "What are we going to do if we run into the tree men again?"

"Fight them," D'Anton said.

"That much I had figured out on my own, thanks. I need a weapon."

D'Anton slid a small knife from his boot and handed it over.

They headed into the forest, Ona's body in full revolt. But what could she do? She wasn't so far gone as to simply lie down in the pine needles and let them kill her. She didn't want to live really, but she also didn't truly want to die. And living was obviously going to take some work.

She took the lead and D'Anton nodded, giving her a tentative smile. His fingers floated over his missing brand. She wished she had some of his newly found happiness to get her through this forest of silver and secrets.

"Happiness doesn't end the dung life brings, but it sure helps clear the air."

"What was that?" D'Anton moved his hair behind his ear. His eyes were warm and his limp was already fading. She was glad to have him in this nightmare with her.

"Oh nothing. I was just being wise. Try to listen next time."

7

KINNERET

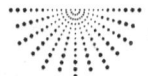

Kinneret scanned the crowd one more time, looking for Oron's familiar tangled locks and cynical face. Nothing. She touched her salt pouch, feeling powerless.

Night descended on the port town of Verita in shades of violet, ocean blue, and blazing yellow. Musicians in bright tunics and caps crept out of every corner. They played lutes, woodwinds, and small drums to those wealthy enough to throw coins. Men in outlandish Silvanian robes sauntered past merchant stands of iced milk. How much did keeping milk frozen cost? Probably enough to feed one thousand low-castes. It was chilly here, but not cold enough to keep ice. Kinneret rolled her eyes, her worry turning to anger. Lanterns glowed from strings across the courtyards leading up to the roads of water.

"Let's search for him, all right? I can't just stand here."

Calev followed her as she hailed a boat. "But where should we look?"

"I don't know. But I'm not twiddling my thumbs while Oron is robbed and beaten to death in some dank alleyway."

"Oron is no stranger to a city full of thieves and roughs. Shouldn't we give him just one night to himself?" Calev's earnest eyes studied her.

"I don't know. He was really upset."

"How about we search for him after we meet the king? We should at least present ourselves. Amir Ekrem expects it. I'm sure Oron will be fine. He probably went to have a drink and kiss a tavern woman."

Kinneret sighed. "Maybe you're right."

They returned to the skiff, where Ridhima handed over the ancient tomes from Ekrem's library and the crate of fresh lemons—gifts for the king.

THE KING'S city castle boasted high walls with arrow slits and pointed arches. A stable full of stomping black horses stood across the inner courtyard from a dock that was somehow fed through an extensive tunnel system that led to the sea.

Kinneret breathed in the scent of the ocean, letting it fill her with confidence.

At the door to the main housing, a guard appeared. His puffy short pants competed with his silk, striped hat for attention. Kinneret settled on the hat. The feather on top really said *regally employed*. She snorted a laugh and Calev elbowed her.

The guard cleared his throat and spoke in a slightly accented version of their language, the trade, or common, tongue. "The king awaits you."

Kinneret didn't think so. Silvania's pompous king wouldn't know the smallest thing about her. "He awaits me?"

"Are you not Kinneret Raza, Amir Ekrem's full-ship kaptan and the liberator of Quarry Isle?"

Calev wiggled his eyebrows. "She is indeed. And my Intended." He winked at the guard, which Kinneret thought was maybe a little over the top. Had he nipped a bit of Oron's wine earlier? "I'm her assistant."

The guard frowned. "If I'm not mistaken, you are also Calev ben Y'hoshua, next Chairman of Old Farm and legendary dagger dancer."

Kinneret laughed hard at Calev's blush, then clapped him on the back. "Yes. The dancing is actually very attractive."

Calev groaned, fully embarrassed now.

"No, really," Kinneret said to the guard. "You should try a good dance instead of that hat. Might grab a nicer form of attention."

The guard blinked, then turned on a heel and stormed into the castle. Without another word to them, he called for servants. A man with grape vines in his hair took the lemon crate while a woman in a bright purple tunic gently accepted the books. One of the books had silver-edged pages and had to be worth a kyros's sum.

A floor of white and gray marble led them through walls of framed mirrors and long windows set high, near the painted ceiling.

"I'm going to hope that somehow that guard didn't understand your little hat comment," Calev said.

Painted rock doves, intricate crowns, chariots, and wild ocean waves crowded the ceiling.

Kinneret whistled at the interior. "Humble fellow, this king."

Calev laughed, his blush finally fading. "Oh yes. A real man of the people," he whispered.

Kinneret's loud laugh startled the guard who walked primly several steps ahead.

The lustrous hallway brought them to a room with gossamer curtains over open windows. The sound of Verita carried on the breeze—boatmen singing for their customers, men and women trading quick words in three different languages, and the clink of coins changing hands. The curtains whipped inward, chasing a sudden gust, and their movement drew Kinneret's and Calev's eyes to the silver gilt throne at the end of the room.

The king stood and opened his arms. "Welcome!" His head nearly brushed the throne's velvet canopy.

His courtiers quieted and turned. Every set of eyes on Kinneret felt like fire pokers. Like somehow they'd know she came from nothing and was only recently raised out of the muck of poverty. But why should she feel ashamed? Pushing those worries aside, she raised her chin and faced those wealthy nobles down.

"Thank you, your highness," Calev said charmingly.

Kinneret bowed, mimicking his movement. "We bring greetings from Amir Ekrem in Jakobden. He hopes our people can be fast friends in these dangerous times."

"Ah. Yes." He motioned to a servant who brought a tray of low, wide glasses to Calev and Kinneret. She took one filled with a dark, red wine. Oron, once again, crossed her mind. She hoped he was simply drinking somewhere and not lying in a gutter. "Please," the king said, "make yourself at home in my castle. We have rooms prepared in the northern wing."

"Our amir sent gifts for you, your highness." Kinneret gestured to the servants behind them.

The king studied the stack of books, murmuring appreciatively. "Very fine indeed." He turned to read the label on the crate. "Old Farm lemons! My dears, gather round. We will all enjoy a slice of the tartness that only the ancient land of Old Farm can produce. You will think yourselves turned inside out with pleasure!"

Calev beamed with pride. Once the group had gushed over their precious lemon slices and questioned Calev about soil types, harvesting times, seed storage, and planting rituals— which the king snickered through obnoxiously—Kinneret decided it was time to move forward.

"Your highness," she said, "if the Invaders strike your territories, Amir Ekrem promises to send—"

"Ah. Ah. Ah." The king held up a finger, then sucked another lemon slice. He puckered his lips and shook his head. "So deliciously tart. Kaptan Kinneret Raza, we will discuss our new friendship tomorrow. After a feast. And some dancing!" He winked at Calev, who grimaced.

As much as she loved seeing Calev charming the court, she couldn't stop worrying about Oron. "We would really like to complete negotiations now, if you don't mind, your greatness."

Calev squeezed the bridge of his nose.

Your greatness might've been a little over the top.

"We would love to feast with you tomorrow before our talks, your highness," Calev said, bowing deeply to the king.

With one more lemon slicing demonstration, the king dismissed Kinneret and Calev. They found themselves outside the castle walls, staring up at a starry sky and still wondering where Oron had gone.

"I'm finished waiting around." Kinneret headed toward a boatman who had a dark green craft at the nearest dock. "We're going after Oron. All right?"

Nodding, Calev hopped into the boat and handed a coin to its master, a man with a wide, upper body and a lean face. "Where can we go to get a good cup of wine?" Calev asked the man.

Kinneret twisted on the boat's seat and looked across the waterway to where it spilled into a larger convergence of liquid roads. There were boats everywhere. So many people. How in the world were they going to find Oron in this if he didn't want to be found?

The boat master lowered his long, wooden pole into the water and pushed them away from the solid ground. "A stretch of taverns run along the western edge of Verita." His accent was strong, his voice deep and rumbling—like most Silvanians. They seemed to exaggerate parts of words which made their version of the Common Tongue sound like a whole new dialect to Kinneret's ears. "You get all sorts in there though," he said. "I'd be careful, if I were in your shoes."

Calev sat beside Kinneret. She took his hand in hers, reveling in the warmth and the familiar calluses. "What if we can't find him?"

"We will. And we'll be back before the Silvanian king misses us tomorrow." Calev's smile lit his face and drove the slight chill in the air away.

Kinneret leaned forward and pressed her mouth to his. His hands drifted over her cheeks and down the column of her neck. His lips followed the path, then he nibbled on her collarbone and sent rivers of goosebumps along her skin. Her entire body warmed. She tangled her fingers in his hair, not caring a bit if the boat master was looking. Calev's touch was the only thing that could shove the fear from her mind and remind her that they'd been through worse than this and would see the other side of this trouble too.

Calev pulled back and a lock of his jet hair fell over his face. His eyes were hot. "We need to marry. Soon."

Her heart lifted. She wanted nothing more. "As soon as we return."

"What about your second mission to Akhayma?"

"There are others better suited and Ekrem will understand."

Calev ran his lips over hers, and she shivered.

"Here we are," the boat master said in his thick Silvanian accent. Kinneret decided she didn't like the sound of it, but he was a good fellow, bringing them here so she stuffed her prejudice out of her mind and gave the master a smile.

The tiny, silver-haired goddess on the boat's prow bobbed as they hopped out and onto a courtyard. A dozen or so taverns sat side-by-side, the ancient buildings like drunken friends leaning heavily on one another. Kinneret passed the boat master a tip.

"So little from those who have so much?" It was an old Silvanian saying and about the only thing Kinneret really could translate. She raised an eyebrow. These boat masters made more in one night than she and Avi had seen in their lifetime—before recent events. Finding the silver on the island of Ayarazi had turned days of aching stomachs and desperation into a blur of filling meals and satisfaction. But she had no desire to hold out on the man. She certainly had enough to go around these days. After giving the man five more coins, she joined Calev, who was already talking to a musician outside a tavern with three arched windows.

"He plays the eagle bone flute, too," Calev was saying. He must've been describing Oron.

The musician shook his head.

Kinneret took Calev's arm. "How about we go in and check?"

"Are you mentally prepared for a load of drunken Silvanians?"

"As I'll ever be."

Though the sun had only just dropped below the horizon, women with rouged cheeks lounged over rich men in every available spot in the tavern. Pushing past a laughing bunch of Silvanian sailors, Kinneret found her way to the barkeep. Calev asked for a bowl of wine.

Kinneret crossed her arms and leaned back on the polished wood of the keep's counter. "Your Silvanian isn't as limited as you led me to believe, Calev ben Y'hoshua."

He shrugged and took the wine from the keep. "I didn't want to make you feel bad."

"It doesn't really. I mean, it's wonderful that you speak it so well, but honestly these people seem like pigs."

Proving her point, the sailors dared one another to drink a bowl of wine in one go. One man spilled half of the red liquid down his front, then belched loud enough to shake the roof.

"I apologize to pigs everywhere," Kinneret said. "These sailors are far worse than any boar I ever met."

"Meet a lot of swine, do you?" Calev's eyes shone over the lip of the wine bowl. He took a sip, then handed it to her.

She accepted it, wishing she had the optimism to joke right

now like Calev did. "We'd have seen him in here by now, don't you think?"

Calev opened his mouth to answer, but the sailors suddenly erupted into a song Kinneret couldn't understand at all. She caught two words she could translate. *Payment* and *Go*.

The group of them sang their way out the tavern door, leaving the place much improved with their absence.

Kinneret finished her portion of the wine and handed it back to Calev. "Let's go to the next tavern. We'll look through all these spots, then we'll head back and double check he didn't return to the king's castle while we were gone."

"As you say, kaptan."

The next tavern was pretty much the same. Women. Sailors. Wine. This one had a quartet of musicians so half the crowd was dancing. After giving Oron's description to countless people and getting nowhere, they headed back toward the king's castle.

Stars glittered overhead, and the air smelled of the sea. Kinneret's feet itched to be back on a boat. Cobblestoned land always felt dead under her feet. She missed the movement of water under her, the way a swell would rise to meet her sandals, forcing her to adjust her stance, to dance to its tune. Like a very determined and bossy friend who demanded respect. That thought brought her back to worrying about Oron.

Where is he? Please be safe, old friend.

A figure swept up beside her. She spun, taking out her dagger.

It was the Northern Isle seithr from earlier—the woman about Kinneret's age with the extremely thick, bluehare cloak she refused to take off despite the mild weather.

"I am no threat." The woman held her staff with its carved

runes like she was offering it to Kinneret. "Your friend. Men took him. Drunken men, sailors, took him to a cursed forest. Payment to gods?"

Kinneret gripped Calev's tunic. "Is she talking about Oron? She is, isn't she?"

Calev just nodded, his mouth open.

Should they trust this seithr? What would be her motivation for lying? To send them into a trap for some reason? It was far-fetched. It made so much more sense that a group of wined-up sailors happened on Oron, who was in a rough state of mind, and the Silvanians decided on some entertainment. It might've been that group from the first tavern.

"What do you know about Silvania's cursed forests?" Kinneret asked Calev. Trees covered most of this country and ran through some of Jakobden and Old Farm too, ignoring human borders.

"Not much. One trader told me about tree spirits in humanlike form. They claim victims for energy. Something like that."

Kinneret hugged herself tightly. She'd heard a story about those forests once too, from a merchant in the tavern beside Jakobden's main port. After she'd stolen a coin from his bag, she'd overheard him talking about how the tree spirits delighted in taking victims, man or woman, who wandered into their depths. One man escaped, but was missing every one of his fingers. She could imagine Oron's strong, able sailor hands being pulled apart, finger by finger.

"We have to find that forest. Now."

"Any Silvanian should know where to find it, right?" Calev eyed the seithr's staff warily. "I'd know if there was a cursed forest near my city."

"I've heard of one, but I have no idea if it's the same one or if that was only a story." A wave of gratitude rose inside Kinneret, briefly tamping down the anger. She touched the impressive seithr briefly on the shoulder. "Thank you," she said in probably the worst version of the Northern Isle tongue ever.

The seithr's deep-set, luminous eyes made her seem older than she had to be. "We," she said, still trying the common tongue, "we are not…perfect."

Kinneret fought back a very cynical laugh at the biggest understatement she'd ever heard. Her people had very little respect for life if the life in question didn't fit their idea of strength and talent. "No, you are definitely not." Maybe this woman could someday change that in her island home. "Far from perfect, but tonight, you're a gift of the Fire. And that makes up for it, just a little bit."

The seithr was obviously finished trying to untangle Kinneret's words because she simply spun and walked off like a kyros, head high.

A couple carrying vats painted with olive designs walked past.

Kinneret jumped in front of them. "Is there a cursed wood near here?" She surprised herself, using passable Silvanian.

The couple pointed toward a wooden sign beyond the next turn on the roads of water. A large boat with tall, maroon sides drifted past, blocking what was written there. Kinneret took off toward the water and finally read the chipped, silver paint.

"Does that say Eastern Woodland Road?"

Calev nodded. "I think it's less than two hours walk from here."

Kinneret's stomach clenched, wondering what they might be doing to Oron. But he was no slouch. He was a fighter.

Hopefully, he'd get away. Doubtful with the odds, but still, it was a possibility. "*When* we find them, my lucky one."

"What are we going to do if we do catch up to them? We have two knives, and your magic doesn't work on dry land—except maybe for healing, right?"

"Right. But we don't have time to get help. If Oron disappears into some nightmare of a forest, Fire only knows what will happen to him. He has risked his life over and over again for Avi, me, and for you, and I won't let anything get in the way of me saving him."

"Even good sense?"

Kinneret unleashed a glare. "We'll figure it out. We always do."

"True."

8

KINNERET

The city's busy water roads and stone pathways gave way to sparse villages. Manor houses loomed on hills dotted with skinny conifers. The villas and farmlands faded, and the dark lines of forests showed on the horizon.

Kinneret stopped to unbuckle her waterskin from her sash. The liquid cooled her throat. The moon was high and traffic on the roadway had dwindled to nothing.

Calev watched the shadows near the scrub growth lining the road. "We can't travel all night. This is dangerous and you know it."

Something small shuffled in the bushes and Kinneret was proud that she didn't jump. It was a bit scary out here at night. They would have a tough time defending themselves if a group of thieves decided to rob them or worse.

"I see your point. If we end up dead, what help are we to Oron? But there aren't exactly a bevy of inns out here."

Calev pointed at a flicker in the distance. "There are charcoal burners. They might put us up until sunrise."

Kinneret's knee-jerk reaction was to grimace at the idea. Everyone knew charcoal burners were an odd bunch. But then again, she was considered pretty odd herself, so she wiped the ugly look off her face and nodded. "Maybe. Just for a few hours." She fixed the waterskin onto her sash.

Calev brushed a piece of hair behind her ear. "You are so sensible these days."

"I'm so dull now that I've grown a brain."

"Dull as sailing through a typhoon."

She smacked him lightly. "Brat."

The charcoal burners' huts huddled beside a line of oaks that swayed in the moonlight. Three huge piles of dirt belched plumes of smoke like doors to the underworld. Men and a few women stood over the charcoal beds.

"Who is it there?" a man called out in a rough version of the trade tongue.

Calev waved. "Two travelers. We hoped we could spend the hours until dawn in one of your homes if it's not too much trouble."

"In our homes?" A woman stepped forward, arms nearly black with charcoal dust.

"Yes," Kinneret said, "if you allow it."

"Such manners for us burners!" The woman laughed and motioned for them to follow her.

The hut the woman led them into was nothing more than four straw mats, a dirt floor, and a thatched roof. The burner gestured to the two mats closest to the door. "Take these. I washed those blankets just yesterday. Sleep as long as you like, travelers. We don't often enjoy the good manners of those who pass us by."

Kinneret's mat was fine. She was well used to sleeping on straw. But sleep didn't want to come. She gave herself a headache staring out the tiny window above Calev and praying for sunrise to come quickly. The moon rose higher still, but the trees blotted its light.

"Calev. I can't do this. I can't sleep while Oron is out there."

He sat up and yawned. "I know. Me either."

Outside of the hut, the woman who'd taken them in smiled from her perch near the burning wood. "No sleep for you?"

"My friend is in trouble," Kinneret said. "I can't rest. We'll have to risk the road and keep on."

Another burner with a long beard studied them. "Where is your friend? Where are you headed?"

Calev closed the hut door and threw the latch to keep it shut. "We believe some drunken sailors took him into a cursed area of the forest."

The burners went very, very still.

"You can't go after him," the woman said. "You will die. The cursed wood is angry. More angry than it has ever been. The animals have acted strangely for a long time. But now, now it is worse."

The other burner tugged at his beard. "We only take fallen wood for our charcoal now. Even here, beyond the cursed boundary. We know better than to anger the forest. You should heed our warning. We've heard stories from the burners south and north of here."

Calev glanced at Kinneret. "What kind of stories?"

"The curse grows stronger. Something foul brews there."

A chill crawled over Kinneret's scalp. "All the more reason to hurry so we can help our friend."

"Well, good luck to you. You will need it," the woman said.

KINNERET DREW close to Calev as they took up their journey down the road. They stayed silent, listening for approaching hooves that would mean either a group of very successful thieves or a group of armed men and women. Silvania seemed to have a lot of those. Though there were strange night insects that called to one another from the trees framing the rocky pathway through the countryside, nothing else seemed to be awake at this hour.

They stopped at a fork in the road.

"Left or right?" Calev asked.

Kinneret looked at her compass. The trees in front of them, not left or right, grew taller than the ones they'd passed so far. Pine scented the night's breeze. A rumble of thunder sounded over that part of the forest and the light of a far-off storm glowed inside towering clouds. "Straight ahead, I think."

Calev's throat moved in a swallow. "Onward."

Off the road, the trees grew thicker and thicker, but just when Kinneret thought the wood might thicken to become a truly deep forest, a cleared area crowded with tree stumps appeared.

Kinneret suddenly wished she had a cloak.

Calev ran a hand over a stump and whispered a prayer.

A plow peeked out from a tangled mess of ivy. Someone had thought to farm here and been persuaded to give up the idea.

Calev shook his head. "They should not have felled these elders."

He was talking about the larger trees that had been cut down. Old Farms always talked about trees like that. Normally, she would've teased him for it, but right now, she completely understood the sentiment in all its layers. The air was heavy and heady. She felt as though she looked out over a field of corpses instead of merely trees. A shiver flew over her shoulders.

"There is something here," she whispered.

Thunder rolled far, far away. Over the wood, the sky flashed a pale orange.

"I think we found the cursed forest." Calev looked beyond the stumps, into the deep, dark green, awe widening his eyes.

This was all somehow worse because there were no drunken sailors to fight. What was here felt so much more dangerous.

Panic flooding her senses, Kinneret cupped her hands at her mouth. Suddenly, she was desperate to find her friend. "Oron!"

A child's voice called from the darker part of the forest. "Help. Please!"

She wasn't certain she'd really heard it.

Then she heard it again. It sounded like a young boy, his words jumbling from the trade tongue into nonsense.

"Please…"

Kinneret and Calev glanced at one another, of the same mind. They needed to find Oron, but they also couldn't just leave some poor child alone in this awful place. Kinneret took off toward the forest, past the felled trees, where the wood resumed its dark reign, Calev just behind her.

"I suppose we'll rescue him too," she said, talking about the boy.

At the line of dark pines and hulking oaks, something sharp wrapped around Kinneret's wrist.

A burning pain seared her flesh, and a scream built in her throat.

Calev helped her tear at the ivy's strange red leaves. The plant didn't seem to burn him like it did her.

When she was free, boils rose along her forearm, her hands, and all the places the ivy had touched. Tears streamed from her eyes. Calev shoved his hair out of his face and gently held her wounded hands as he looked around frantically. Kinneret focused on controlling the pain. Fainting in a cursed forest probably wasn't the best idea.

"Help!" the boy shouted again.

Kinneret scanned the trees for him, but pain overtook the search as Calev dragged her through more pines and tall oaks to another treeless expanse.

"There." Calev pointed to a silver pond that lay among the fallen leaves and pine needles. "You can rinse off."

Like the moon had poured half itself onto the earth, the water shone brightly, still and eerie in the night.

"Go in. The leaves must hold some oil that your skin doesn't tolerate. I've seen such a thing at Old Farm. Little Kinsey can't touch the greenery around the well. Gets boils like this every time she does."

Almost dizzy with pain, Kinneret stepped into the pool. The water hissed around her wounds as she dipped them beneath the cloudy surface. This water didn't feel like water usually did. But the pain dissipated. She sighed in relief.

A soft voice carried on the wind. It wasn't the boy. This was a male voice. A man. But it wasn't Oron. The words layered on top of other words and other voices. They weren't in any language she'd heard, but somehow Kinneret knew they were asking her to go to them.

Come. Strong one. Rise. I wait.

Kinneret swallowed and fought the pull. "Did you hear that?"

Calev cocked his head, then nodded. "Oron?" he called out, his voice tentative.

He held his hands out to Kinneret and she took them, climbing out of the water. Her skirt clung to her legs, so she shook the fabric out. The welts on her arms had faded completely, but she didn't feel healed. Something in that water...

A crash sounded in the wood and both of them raised their knives.

A big, well-muscled man and a limping woman with a fierce face emerged from the trees. They shouted something in Silvanian and gestured toward the silver pool. Then the woman noticed Kinneret's wet clothing. She pressed her lips together, then touched the man's arm and nodded toward Kinneret. The man let out a rush of Silvanian.

Kinneret finally figured out what he was asking.

"Were you blessed or cursed?"

9

ONA

Ona switched to using the trade language, her arms shaking from the pain in her wound and the fear of the tree men returning. She and D'Anton had tried to escape the forest the way they'd come, but the clearing of tree stumps was nowhere to be found. It was fairly obvious this was a part of the wood's curse. "Were you blessed or cursed by the silver pool?"

The woman with the dark, red-brown hair answered. "Blessed, I think. Some ivy...it burned my skin. The water cleaned it away and healed my wounds." Her voice was strong, but she wouldn't make eye contact so she was either seeing Ona and D'Anton as potential enemies or she was hiding something.

The man with her was obviously an Old Farm. The sash tied around his trim waist boasted embroidered barley and bright lemons. His hair held the imprint of a headtie though he must've lost it somewhere along the way. He was a very fine-looking man with his sleek, jet-colored hair and laughing eyes.

The way he angled his body toward the woman showed his strong attraction to her. Ona would've bet every man, and a few women, had glanced her way.

D'Anton clasped forearms with the other man, then with the woman. He told them their names and they did the same.

Ona's mouth popped open. She spoke quickly, knowing the green men could return at any moment. "You're Kinneret Raza, the one who took down the Oramiral?" This Pass Witch had raised the seas to do her dirty work and kill that disgusting slaver on Quarry Isle. How could someone so powerful be stuck here? "Why aren't you on the Pass, working for your new amir?"

"I *am* working for Amir Ekrem." Kinneret raised her chin proudly.

Ona didn't blame her. The sailor should be proud. She'd done something no one in history had accomplished. And she'd taken the formerly low-caste ability to work sea salt and prayers and turned it into a magic everyone in the South wished they possessed. The Salt Witch touched a small bag tied to her sash. That must've been where she kept her salt. Ona was seriously impressed. Too bad they were far from the sea in this place of nightmares.

"Amir Ekrem sent us here to negotiate an agreement with your king." Kinneret eyed D'Anton.

He tugged at his tunic and watched the surrounding branches, the shadows between the pines and the gnarled roots of the hulking oak trees. Without his Invader surcoat, his clothing was plain enough that it could be from anywhere really. Ona wasn't about to divulge D'Anton's secrets. He'd saved her from a fate worse than death, a life inside some cursed tree. Who knew what pain she would've endured in there? Without D'Anton's help, she wouldn't have had the chance to someday find Lucca and Seren, to find a way to make up for what she'd done. But would these two find out that D'Anton was an Invader? If they did, it would come to blows. Ona was positive she didn't have the strength to fight them, then battle more tree men.

A good twist of the truth was in order. "D'Anton here helped me escape from a band of rogue Invaders, who'd also taken him." Oh, but he had an Invader name. How could she explain that? "But he was taken as a child. They raised him there. That's why he has an Invader name. He is actually Silvanian."

D'Anton's gaze flew to Ona, but she kept her eyes focused on Kinneret. He had to be Silvanian. What was he so upset about? Why hide it now? Whatever. At least this hidden truth would help him keep this legendary sailor's ire off his back.

Kinneret studied Ona's face. Ona felt exposed, almost wishing she had her sword. This witch was nothing short of terrifying. The woman cocked her chin in a way that said she knew Ona was twisting the truth. Ona had heard Kinneret grew up on the streets of Jakobden and such a rough upbringing probably taught her to read people better than most. There was something about her, something that made Ona want to fight her best again. The corner of her own mouth lifted, and it surprised her.

She realized then that D'Anton had been watching her. He gave Ona a small smile that unexpectedly flipped Ona's stomach. She blinked, then turned away quickly. At least he didn't seem angry about her story of his past.

Now that she was fairly certain these Jakobden folk weren't going to murder D'Anton, Ona broached the terrible topic that was most important to their survival in this cursed forest.

"Kinneret. Calev. There are men who seem to be part of the forest. Their arms and faces...it's hard to explain. It's like they're part tree."

Her throat thickened. She wasn't ready to tell them about being inside a tree for those brief minutes. The smell of rotting wood. The feel of the bark crawling up her legs. The tightness in her chest.

"They're called green men," she added, "and they're controlled by some sort of god of this dark wood. I've heard about them in stories, but I had no idea they could be real. They attacked me. And D'Anton. You should be on your guard at every second. We tried to escape, but the way we came in isn't there anymore."

D'Anton led the group down another path on this side of the silver pool. "This way seems to go in a similar direction to the way we came in, so maybe it'll lead us out," he suggested. "Where did you two enter the forest?"

Calev spun his dagger, then held it at the ready, his other hand floating near Kinneret's body like he had to be near her all the time. "I've heard tales about the cursed forests of Silvanian." His eyes were wide as he looked up into the arms of an oak as tall as the entrance to Akhayma's walls. The sheer scale of this wood was mind-blowing. "We came in through a field that had been stripped of both elders and young ones."

The Old Farm's face was serious and reverent, full of mourning, but what did he mean by *elders and young ones*?

"He's talking about mature trees and saplings," Kinneret said. "It's an Old Farm thing." She waved off any questions Ona might've had. "Anyway, there was an area where some enterprising farmer had cleared the trees."

"That's where we ran in, too." Ona touched her wound gingerly.

D'Anton pulled three leaves from his pocket and popped them into his mouth. His face bunched a little as he chewed, most likely making a medicinal paste for Ona. The plant must've tasted horrible.

"You don't have to do that for me," she said.

"I know." He glanced her way and pushed his hair behind an ear.

A wave of gratitude swept over her and she hated it. She didn't deserve his kindness. She was a monster. Suddenly Ona found herself on the ground panting. Three faces stared down at her as emotions raged around her heart, weighing her down, drowning her.

The dagger D'Anton had given her lay beside her right leg. She must've dropped it. "I'm fine."

Kinneret knelt and pulled a small amount of salt from her pouch. The salt on her fingers twinkled in the scant moonlight through the leaves. "I might be able to heal you a little. I'm not sure, but I'll try."

Ona moved her clothing away from the scabbed wound and D'Anton pressed the paste gently against the skin there. His thumb brushed her collarbone. Her breath caught in her throat. Kinneret's hands were on her then, very warm and confident. The witch began to whisper about the sea's tie to the earth, about healing and light, about life flowing. It sounded ridiculous and beautiful at the same time.

A cluster of dark leaves snaked over Kinneret's shoulder and pulled her back.

Ona's heart dropped.

Calev shouted and lashed his dagger at the living branch. The darkness cloaked the body and face of the creature.

Ona angled herself at the thing's dead side and jabbed her blade up and in, aiming for the lungs and praying the thing had organs to injure.

D'Anton disappeared into the black forest.

Kinneret's hands hung at her sides as the creature drew her backward. Her eyes glazed over, unseeing.

The green man's face appeared in a column of moonlight, and he nearly looked human. Leaves unfurled at the end of his eyelashes and his voice was soft—

Calev shouted Kinneret's name and the sound shook Ona awake. He lunged to strike. His dagger seemed to hit just under the tree spirit's arm, but the creature didn't even flinch.

D'Anton appeared behind the creature and dragged the runed sword across the thing's neck, just above Kinneret's head. The green man shrieked and that soft, lulling voice shattered into wails crowding Ona's ears.

Kinneret's eyes cleared, and she bit down on the thing's branchlike arm. It didn't let go.

The deafening noise increased.

Ona dropped back and covered her head with her arms, her dagger forgotten. She was no warrior anymore. All her muscle memory was gone. No. Despite the change in her, she would fight for this proud, amazing woman. She wouldn't cower here in fear.

Shaking off the terror as best she could, Ona leapt at Kinneret's foot. She latched on as the shrieking creature dragged them both into a circle of star shine and oak trees. Kinneret looked down at Ona, but the famed sailor wasn't herself. A darkness blacker than ink, colder than midnight, deeper than any forgotten cave, cloaked the whites of her eyes and the color of her irises. She was lost to the forest.

A memory flowed through Ona's mind as she clutched onto Kinneret's leg, digging in her nails. Calev tried to force the creature down and D'Anton sliced at its legs.

Time slowed. Ona's thoughts slipped away.

Her mind showed an image of the last mural she'd painted with her aunt, before the Invader attack that destroyed her life and turned it all to hate and vengeance. The mural stretched over the western wall of her aunt's villa. On it, women and men in flowing, amethyst robes danced around a sparkling fire of white and blue and orange. Trees grew around the borders—Ona had yet to detail the pines' fine needles—and one special pine showed the faint outline of a slanted smile. That grin had always bothered her. When her aunt had first sketched it and chalked it, she'd asked why it had to be there. There was, of course, a reason, because her aunt did nothing without good reason. She'd been a sensible one despite being an imaginative artist. Ona remembered the sorrow in her aunt's eyes when she explained.

"You know Silvania has its cursed forests here and there," Ona's aunt had said that day so long ago. "They demand sacrifices. We must paint as it is, not as we want it to be."

Her aunt had never again mentioned the curse or anything about tree spirits, but Ona had heard the stories from other children her age.

She shook off the memory to see time speed up again.

The wood's soft, sickly whispers hounded her, though the shrieking had stopped. The spirit still had Kinneret in its arms, but she was fighting, thrashing, her shape and the tree creature's blurring and blending in the dark. It didn't seem to be hurting her though, just holding her and pulling her toward a massive pine. Ona gave one last wrenching twist to Kinneret's leg and the witch shouted something at the same moment.

She broke free.

With a shout from Calev, all four of them were running through the night-cloaked forest. Branches scratched Ona's cheeks. Her wound pulsed in time with her racing heart. Roots and scrub grabbed her feet, and she stumbled time and time again, only to feel Kinneret's hand on her arm, D'Anton's fingers bracing against her back in support, or Calev's head turned to check and make sure she was getting back up. She ran for herself, but she also ran for them. Here were good folk that didn't deserve to die in a cursed wood and she would do her very best not to fail good men and women ever again. Considering her past, it was the least she could do.

The pines and oaks gave way to a stretch of maples and sycamores along a bubbling river. They stopped, everyone panting. The scent of sweat, last year's musky leaves, and clean water filled Ona's nose.

"Back to back." D'Anton made a circle motion with his hand and held his etched sword high. "Ona, you rest in the middle of us. Take a breath. Then we'll move on."

"Agreed," Kinneret and Calev said together.

"So these are tree spirits." Kinneret nodded like she was trying to convince herself.

Ona shared her memory and the awful, and painfully vague, bits about sacrifice.

Kinneret whispered something and stood a little closer to Calev. "We have to find him."

"Our friend, Oron," Calev said, "was taken here by a group of—"

"Mules who'd had more than their share of drink and will definitely wish they'd never been born to this life if I get my hands on them." Kinneret gestured with her dagger.

The woman had been in fights, but she most likely had no formal training. She moved with the knowledge of what strikes could kill and maim, but without the grace of a true warrior.

Ona stood, tired of being the one everyone had to care for. She dusted herself off and joined the circle. "We can get him back. D'Anton's sword works well against them."

He ran a hand over the symbols shining eerily in the steel. "I found it here. In the forest. It's etched with runes."

The sun was rising, throwing pink at tree trunks and along the ripples in the small river flowing beside them. The strands of deep brown and pale yellow shone in D'Anton's hair. Kinneret's skin, light brown and lovely, became paler and rougher toward her hands. Maybe that was from sailing, from the rough work on lines and with the sea water always leeching the moisture from her. Calev's bright green tunic pulled against the muscles in his leg as he leaned to look at the weapon.

Calev took the sword from D'Anton and examined the runes. "I wondered why yours worked and mine didn't. It couldn't just be the size."

"Oron would've made a rough joke about now." Kinneret's eyes looked wet. She cleared her throat and sighed. "What happened right after that tree spirit grabbed me? I have a blank spot in my memory of it, although I guess it could just be the fact that I was being maimed by a tree, for Fire's sake."

Ona tucked her blade into her belt and accepted a small strip of dried meat from D'Anton. "Your eyes went blank. You stopped fighting the creature."

She glanced toward Calev, who nodded and stared at the

meat D'Anton had given him like he had no appetite. "I remember feeling the tightness at my throat. Then the whispering. This will sound like madness, but did the loudest, clearest voice sound…pleasant?"

Ona knew exactly what she meant. That was how she felt when the whispers gathered into one voice and spoke directly to her. "Yes. I wanted to follow the voice. That one voice."

Kinneret was a little green around the mouth as she studied her rough hands. She curled her fingers tight and closed her eyes for a breath. "I can still hear it."

She could? "Does anyone else?" Ona asked.

Calev and D'Anton shook their heads. Calev watched Kinneret very, very closely. He ran a thumb over her elbow. His gaze went to her fisted hands and she put them behind her back.

"I don't think they're chasing us right now. Let's look for Oron," Kinneret said.

"I can do some tracking." The edge of D'Anton's mouth lifted and his eyebrows rose.

"Where did you learn?" Ona remembered Lucca's stories of tracking when he was a child. He told her a tale about following a herd of deer and nearly toppling off a waterfall in his excitement to tell his brother when he spotted them.

Kinneret whirled and smiled at D'Anton. "Please. Get on with it with all my blessings. If we find him, you can have a position on my full-ship if you choose."

D'Anton's eyebrows rose to his hairline. "Thank you." He bowed slightly, then faced Ona. "I learned from my father. It's the only thing he ever did for me." Crouching, he ran fingers over a spot on the forest floor.

Exhausted and sharing what little food they had, the group

wove through the forest. It seemed like this Oron fellow was Kinneret's right hand man as well as a sort of father figure. The old Ona would've argued to forget about Oron and focus on getting out of here, but this new Ona heard Seren's voice in her ear, felt her kindness in her heart. Seren would've died before she left an innocent man in a forest full of monsters. Although Ona could never be good, she could at least try, at this moment, to do the right thing.

"This is for you, Seren, and you, Lucca," she whispered.

D'Anton stopped. His hands fell to his sides. "What did you say?" He turned slowly.

"Nothing. I was just...nothing." Ona's wound was definitely better, but pain still thrummed through the area as constant as a horse's gait on a long journey.

"You said *Lucca*."

The way he said it—it sounded different from the way she'd always pronounced her best friend's name. Not wildly altered. Just different. This was how that name was meant to be said. She knew it, somehow. A shiver rolled over her.

"Yes. He is my friend. Was my friend."

D'Anton was in her face in a blink. "Who are you?"

"I am, well, I *was* a mercenary. I fought with a group. Although I never met the king or any nobles, we worked for them all at one time or another. You know how it is." D'Anton was from Silvania. He knew about the trouble between the nobles and the king, and how mercenaries hired themselves out to the highest bidder. "I met Lucca in a forest on the other side of Silvania. Near my village. I—"

"Black, curly hair? Lost a brother?"

And then she knew.

Her knees wobbled.

This was Lucca's runaway brother, Dante.

She gripped his arms, digging her fingers into the cloth and flesh, and studied his face for a resemblance to her dearest friend. Her heart cinched tightly with a mix of joy and sadness. The likeness showed in the deep set of the eyes and the slant of the shoulders and the chin. She hugged Dante close and fought the urge to cry.

10

KINNERET

Kinneret didn't want to break up this reunion or whatever it was, but Oron wasn't getting any more rescued.

She touched Ona's back. This D'Anton—or Dante—fellow seemed just fine with her all over him, but they needed to move. "If your friend Lucca was trapped in this wood, you wouldn't waste any time. Can we please continue tracking?"

Ona turned, nodding, and wiped her eyes. "I'm being an idiot. Sorry. I just..." She looked at Dante with new eyes. "You're his brother. He *has* to see you."

Dante looked shaken. "So he's alive?"

"I hope so. He was inside the city when you attacked, but you lost the battle. So there is a good chance he lives still. He is close with the new kyros, Seren."

Kinneret held up her hands. "Wait. When *you attacked?* Dante is not an Invader. You can't be an Invader." It wasn't a question. He couldn't be. Invaders were bloodthirsty and insane. Dante was kind and helpful and nothing like the Invaders she'd heard about.

Or maybe he was just very good at acting.

Calev had a knife against Dante's side before Kinneret could suggest it. She loved Calev more every day.

"You better answer well, or you'll find your spleen at your feet," Calev whispered.

Dante nodded. "Just my spleen? No other internal organs will be damaged?"

"I can be merciful."

Dante raised an eyebrow. "You do realize I'm twice your size and have fought professionally for more years than you've been a man?"

Calev spoke through gritted teeth. "I don't have a problem skewering an old man if the old man is an Invader."

"I'm twenty and four."

Ona's hair tumbled out of its ties. "Stop. Ugh." She pushed her fallen hair over her shoulders. "Stop with the pissing contest, you two. Dante was an Invader, but he isn't now."

This made no sense to Kinneret. "But he is Silvanian. I'm so confused."

Dante eyed Calev's blade. "I ran away from home at thirteen. My father was a violent man. He never hurt my mother or brother, but he was an absolute terror to me, his disappointing first born. I made it into the Empire, then a rogue pack of Invaders captured me and took me to the West. I was forced to learn their language, train with them, and was branded as one."

Kinneret grabbed his collar and tugged it down. "I don't see any brand."

"The silver pool erased it," Dante said. "I was blessed."

Hmm. That could've been a lie. "And exactly how did you two meet?"

Ona took over. "His cohorts captured me after I was seriously wounded. When they realized they didn't have any cards to play or wars to fight, they decided to chop me up into bits for the fun of it. Dante helped me escape."

"That does prove some honor." Calev lowered his weapon.

Kinneret studied Ona. She was well-muscled like a fighter, but she didn't defend herself like one. "If you were a mercenary, why aren't you fighting like one?" Kinneret had seen ten-year-olds fight better than Ona had against that tree man.

Ona paled. "I'm not who I was before my injury."

"Fine. Well, it's great you found one another and perhaps you can head on back to wherever this Lucca is once we get out of here, but let's find my innocent friend now, all right?"

In terse agreement, Dante took up tracking again. He halted to touch the ground or a tree branch every now and then. The rest kept their weapons raised, ready to defend themselves against the tree spirits if the creatures decided to attack.

Kinneret stayed behind Dante, eyeing his movements. Was he truly tracking? Was he motivated enough to do this right? "Have you seen anything definitive?"

Dante lifted a broken branch, then tossed it down. "This place is riddled with activity. The green men are everywhere. Their feet...if you can call them that...seem to be more root than anything, and they leave different marks. I've seen no less than five human footprints. One small. An older child. The other is from a heavier adult with unusually rounded feet. How big is this friend of yours?"

Kinneret described Oron.

Dante led them into a grove of thick-bodied pines. A fog

that definitely wasn't normal ghosted toward them and cloaked the wide branches and dark leaves.

Everyone froze.

The branches of the pines were so tangled and full of needles that the morning sun failed to break through, casting only a weak glow over the foggy grove.

The air was even heavier here than the rest of the wood. Kinneret had almost grown used to the weighty feel of the cursed place, but this, this was so much more. It pressed on her shoulders and caressed her cheeks with resin-scented moisture.

A tingling pressure slid up Kinneret's fingers and into her arms. She'd tried not to look at her hands during the last hours because the water had done something odd to them and she didn't really want to think about what it meant. The skin had gone moon white and an uneven texture spread along the backs of her hands and along the sides of her forearms up to her elbows. Now, the white was fading into a silvery brown.

Like the skin of a pine.

"Took you long enough," a voice croaked from somewhere to the right.

Kinneret's chest caved in.

A long, wide crack marred an ancient tree, and Oron looked back at her from inside.

She ran to him, the rest on her heels. "Oron! Are you all right?"

"Yes," he whispered hoarsely. Half his face was covered by the tree, like the thing had simply grown up around him. Only his right side remained exposed to the world. "I'm feeling quite grand. Though I am glad you're here. These tree spirits aren't the best company. They don't laugh at any of my jokes, and if you can believe it, they don't have a stitch of wine."

Calev and Kinneret both latched onto the bark near Oron's nose and began trying to break him free.

"Why did you go off on your own? That was truly stupid. I shouldn't even bother rescuing your stubborn tail." Anger made it easier for Kinneret to keep from screaming and being completely worthless with panic. "It was those drunk Silvanian sailors that took you, wasn't it? I knew they were trouble."

"It was them. And yes, I am truly stupid. But one cannot judge matters of the heart with the same law as one does...ah, never mind. Just get me out of here, please."

Calev grimaced and pulled again. Ona and Dante joined them in trying to rip the pine apart.

The wood groaned like a person. Everyone pulled their hands away from the tree.

Oron swallowed with difficulty. "I don't think force is going to work. This escape of mine needs a bit of drama."

Then, as if the forest was waiting for its cue to speak, that soft, honeyed voice slithered into Kinneret's ears.

I await your arrival, strong one. I am Runnos. We will be as one.

A feeling like gentle but strong hands floated over Kinneret's body and up into her hair, along her scalp. She swallowed and rubbed her ears, trying to get the sounds out of her head. Her heart pounded like she'd jumped off Amir Ekrem's full-ship and into a cold ocean.

"Did everyone hear that?" The rest of them looked at her blankly. "Guess not."

Calev's eyes widened. "Kin. What is happening to your hands?" He took them and ran his fingers over the rough skin and oddly colored flesh.

"I think I had some sort of reaction to that water. In the silver pool."

"Cursed." Ona frowned, looking Kinneret up and down.

Oron tried to cough, but didn't seem able to expand his chest enough to do the job. "That voice—that'll be the god of the wood, Runnos, unless I'm mistaken. Real piece of work. I've heard them speak of him. Has big plans. I think you, Kinneret, will have to say hello if I have any chance of shedding this rather uncomfortable new outfit. There is a boy who lives in this forest. Near the spring. I think you should try to find him too if you can. He is a strange one, but he seems to know exactly where the tree spirits gather. He may be able to give us some hints on how to deal with Runnos."

Kinneret ignored the bit about herself. "Fire and sea! I forgot about the boy. Calev and I heard him calling for help before the attack."

"I heard a boy too. When we first entered the forest." Ona swallowed. "I'd decided it was one of the forest's tricks, but maybe not. Maybe he *was* trying to get some help for you, Oron. We'll have to get him out of here too."

Oron groaned a little, then coughed. "Yes. That's probably him. I've only heard snippets about him from the voices in the trees."

Calev's eyes flashed. "What does Runnos want with Kinneret, Oron? You said you think she must say hello to him."

"His green men…that's what they call themselves in my head…anyway, they said he has been waiting for one such as you. Sounds ominous, doesn't it? But maybe you can just have a nice chat about what they're all so worked up about and gain my freedom."

"They're upset about something?" Kinneret tore a strip from the bottom of her skirt, soaked it in water from the pouch attached to her sash, and stretched high to reach Oron. She worked the dripping cloth toward his mouth.

Oron struggled to sip from the fabric. He couldn't move his head much. Kinneret fought tears and gave him the bravest smile she could muster. He closed his one visible eye in thanks, and she climbed back down.

Calev's mouth became a line. "Runnos and his tree men, they must be angry about the trees that were felled. It's an offense against this sacred forest. I knew it."

Dante unsheathed his rune-etched sword. "Should I use this to try to free Oron?"

"That is a fancy piece of steel." Oron's one visible eye moved. "And for the record, I vote *Yes*."

Calev crossed his arms. "I don't know. It might anger the spirits more if you do."

Kinneret squeezed Calev's shoulder. "Let's try to find the boy and see if he can give us some insight on Runnos in exchange for helping him escape this place along with us. Then, we can go to Runnos and I'll bargain for Oron's freedom. Maybe if I promise to punish the Silvanians who cut the trees down in the clearing and make sure it doesn't happen again, the god will release you," she said, touching the bark near Oron's face. "I think Calev is right. If we just cut you out with this sword, the creatures might simply pop out of their trees and take us down. It's not the smart move."

Ona nodded. "I will stay here with Oron if you wish. I can keep the rune-etched sword in case all goes wrong. That way you'll have Dante and Calev to fight at your side if Runnos attacks. If I hear your scream, I'll cut him free, and we'll do our best to get to you with the runed weapon."

Kinneret traded a look with Calev. She didn't love this. Not at all. Neither did he, she could tell. But Ona's plan was a good one. Calev was already nodding.

"Thank you," Kinneret said. "Now Dante, do you think you can find this spring Oron is talking about?"

"I can find water. If it's that certain spring, I don't know. But I can find the water."

"Too bad you can't find a convenient little sea. Then I'd have this Runnos on his knees." It was frustrating that her magic only worked on salt water. She set a hand against Oron's head. "Stay strong, friend. I'll do what I can. If it all fails, I will die trying to get you out of here."

A rumbling echoed through the wood. The ground vibrated under Kinneret's sandals. "What is that?"

Before anyone could answer, a crowd of animals charged into the grove.

Rabbits scurried underfoot. Birds blackened the fog. Deer rushed past, bumping against Kinneret's sides and blocking her view of the others. Ona screamed, and Kinneret glimpsed Dante as he raced to the mercenary's side.

11

ONA

A stag's antlers tore across Ona's side and ripped her undershirt and the flesh underneath. Heat and pain poured through her ribs. She fell against the tree. Dante was there before she knew she'd called out, and his body shielded her from the torrent of fleeing animals. Huddled at the base of the tree trunk, she grabbed the toe of one of Dante's boots like it was an anchor that would keep her safely in place.

Finally, the rush of animals faded into a few foxes and a hawk. Dante knelt and moved her arm gently to see her wound. His fingers touched her lightly here and there as the wounded area pulsed with pain and buzzed with numbness.

His lips drew in. "I don't think your ribs are broken. But they are bruised badly and you have a pretty good cut. Why must you insist on getting hurt every few minutes?" He gave her a wry grin as he scoured the ground, presumably searching for more of his healing plants.

"I like to keep it interesting."

"I thought I had the interesting part covered, thank you very much," Oron snapped from above.

Dante spoke to Kinneret and Calev. "What was that all about? Any ideas?"

Now that Ona knew he was Lucca's brother, she saw it in every move and word. He was so Lucca. But he was also just Dante. Similar, but so, so different. She'd never wanted to study the slope of Lucca's forehead and the way he moved his mouth when he was worried. Not like she studied Dante. Point in fact, she really couldn't stop staring at this runaway with the complicated past.

Ona hissed as Dante pressed something green against her side. "Maybe they're off to say hello to Runnos as well?" she said, gritting her teeth.

Calev shrugged and turned his sun-browned face toward Kinneret. "Did you hear his voice just then?"

"No," Kinneret said, "but their activity must be tied to his presence and his anger at the cleared part of his sacred wood. It makes sense, right?"

"Unless we're about to be consumed by a massive forest fire." Calev sniffed the air like he might suddenly smell the source of such a blaze.

Kinneret eyed Ona. "Well, Dante must stay here now. You can't defend Oron when you're bleeding in not one but two places. I want Oron protected by the best fighter we have here. Right now, that's Dante."

"Plus," Dante said, "I'm the only one familiar enough with the plants here to find something that will help Ona heal further."

Ona hated this weakness in herself. They were right. Dante would have to stay.

Dante nodded. "The spring will be up there somewhere." He pointed through the grove, toward an area that was covered in ridged stone. "Look for heavy moss on the rocks and you should find it. If you don't, come right back here and I'll go out and find it."

Ona was disgusted with herself. Where was her ferocity? Her spirit? Her ability? She was so frail now. Like a spring flower, trampled and not strong enough to face the summer heat.

Kinneret and Calev gave them one last wave, then disappeared into the trees.

Dante settled himself at the base of the tree that held Oron and supported Ona's back. He laid the sword across his lap and kept a keen watch on the trees, his gaze moving with every snap of a branch or coo of a bird. Ona was watching his pulse beat against the skin under his jawline when he spoke quietly.

"What is my brother like?" He turned his gray eyes to her, and she froze.

"He is my best friend."

The edge of Dante's mouth lifted. "I'm glad, but I don't know you well, so the fact tells me little."

"Good point. I'm not who I was."

"And who was that?"

"A ruthless mercenary who wanted only revenge and didn't care what she destroyed on her way to getting that revenge."

"Cheerful," Oron said from above.

Ona had thought he was sleeping or whatever one did stuck inside a magic tree. "Right. Well, I did crack some jokes from time to time." She hoped her heavily accented trade tongue was understandable.

"Did you hurt Lucca?" Dante's tone wasn't really accusatory, just curious.

"Yes. Emotionally, not physically."

"The kyros?" Oron's voice squeaked. "You know what? I'm just going to try to pass out for a bit. This is all a little too much."

"Can we get you anything?" Dante twisted to look up.

"No. Go on with the get-to-know-you. I'll be fine."

"He is brave," Ona said. It had to be painful in there.

Dante agreed. "What does my brother have to do with the kyros?"

"The Empire deemed Seren, Kyros Meric's wife, the new kyros when he died. She is the reason the Invaders lost."

"Did she come up with those exploding containers?" Dante swallowed.

"Along with an engineer, yes."

"Genius." His voice was grim.

"She and Lucca truly care for one another."

Dante's eyes widened and he looked at his lap.

She didn't blame him for being amazed that a Silvanian mercenary could attach himself to a kyros. "It is pretty shocking. A lot of the higher ups weren't too thrilled with the affair."

"I can imagine. Lucca doesn't seem like a kyros's spouse."

"I disagree. He isn't overly authoritative, but he is a good leader when he has to be. He has a level head and an open mind. I guess it comes from reading all those books."

"He still does that?" Dante grinned and smoothed a hand over his knee, toying with a tear in the fabric. "I was never much for books."

"You and the old me would've got along nicely."

"Not the new you?"

Ona touched the closest rune on the end of the sword. Two slanted lines came together above a circle. "Maybe. I'm just not sure who the new me is."

"I understand." He stared into the grove as the mist thickened around them. "I thought my life was set in stone, that I would be who the Invaders wanted me to be until I found death. But now," he touched the place where his brand once was, "the world is open and I'm lost on what to do with this second chance."

"Exactly. I thought I was dead on that battlefield. I've lost my will to fight and I was a mercenary. I've never been anything else. What good is a mercenary who can't chant?"

"You can chant."

"So can Lucca."

"I would've liked to see him do that."

"You will. You can return to Akhayma with me. If we get out of here alive."

Dante's face changed. His light brown eyebrows moved toward his hairline and his eyes sparked. "You would travel with me? After we tried to kill you and my brother?"

"The Invaders tried to kill us. And it's not like you had a choice, Dante."

"You always have a choice," Oron mumbled.

Ona scowled. "I thought you were asleep."

"I am."

Dante waved a dismissive hand at Oron. "So you don't hate me, Ona?"

"You saved my life."

"Not at first. At first I was your captor."

A horrible thought sprinted through her mind. "Were you the one who ran me through?"

"No. I didn't see you until the end. We gathered you up."

Ona exhaled. "So you didn't try to kill me. Not directly. And I think that's as good as it can get in our situation." Ona laughed to herself.

"What's so funny?"

"Lucca and I make up terrible mottos for ourselves sometimes. That one would be a solid choice. *As good as it can get in our situation!* Great motivator right there."

Dante chuckled. "I think my brother still has his sense of humor."

"He definitely does."

"Does he look like me? I haven't seen him in so long and he was just a boy when I ran away…"

Ona's gaze slid over Dante's strong, dimpled chin and his furrowed brow. "Some, yes. But your eyes are light and his are dark. His hair is nearly black. Your hair is lighter and has a load of other colors in it like copper…" She reached out to touch a strand, then realized what she was doing and pulled her hand back.

He grabbed it gently. "It's all right. It's amazing to have someone being kind to me." His jaw tensed. "Sorry. I'm acting like a child."

"You're not. I'm sure those Invaders weren't real sweethearts."

He laughed a little. "No, they were not."

She ran her fingers down the side of his face. His eyes closed. "You are among friends now, Dante. I may not be able to help you fight, but I am here. Whoever I am."

Opening his eyes, he smiled. "I'm glad."

12

KINNERET

Kinneret led Calev up the small rise, climbing over tree roots and hoping she wouldn't hear that voice inside her head again anytime soon. She'd much rather meet this forest god and talk to him face-to-face. She'd negotiated and/or stolen almost everything she'd eaten or possessed since birth up until this past moon cycle and this creature skulking around in her head wasn't about to get the best of her. Haggling was as natural as swimming.

"What do we have to bargain with?" she asked. Brainstorming with Calev always produced good ideas.

"With all the talking he is doing inside your head, it seems like Runnos wants you, specifically, to do something for him. I wonder if he ends up having to force you to do whatever he wants, if it might mess with the magic of whatever it is."

"That's a load of whatevers. So you think he might need to persuade me to do this mysterious whatever willingly or it won't take?"

"Maybe."

"Do you think the farmer who originally cleared the land is dead?"

Calev shrugged. "That would be my guess."

"Maybe we can threaten Runnos with more clearing?" The fog snaking around the trees lessened and sunlight speared the leafy canopy. "Other landowners would be interested if we word things in a certain way. Silvania doesn't have a lot of land to divvy up, right?"

"True," Calev said. "But Runnos might say he can strike down those who try to cut more of the forest."

A root tripped Kinneret, and she hissed at the pain in her toe as she regained her footing. "There are a lot of humans in Silvania. He can't possibly kill them all."

"We have numbers on our side." Calev set a hand on a pine and climbed over an outcropping of mossy rock. "And persistence. Motivation. We aren't giving up Oron or you. We'll die first."

Kinneret snorted. "But will the rest of Silvania sacrifice themselves for us? I don't think so."

"Of course not. But Runnos doesn't have to know that," Calev whispered, tugging at Kinneret's skirt.

He *had* learned a little about negotiating from her, she thought proudly. "We also have that sword with the runes inscribed on it. Dante's sword."

"It slices through these cursed trees like a hot knife in butter."

Kinneret rubbed her hands together, getting excited. "Exactly. He won't want us waving that thing around."

Her fingers caught on one another and she paused, staring at them and turning them over and over.

Her skin was changing again.

Her fingernails faded into tapered ends like branches and a tiny bud pressed out of her wrist.

She sucked a breath.

Calev grabbed her and looked around for what might've injured her. "What is it?"

"My hands. Look." There was no hiding this now.

Calev's lips parted as he touched her fingers gently. "My Kinneret. My fire. What is he doing to you?"

Tugging her hands away and trudging onward, she raised her chin and fought tears of panic. "We will fix it. We've been through worse than this."

Behind her, Calev took a loud, strengthening breath before he started walking.

"We certainly have." His words were steel and blood. "And we have won."

WATER BUBBLED from a slide of rocks near a slender path between ferns. At the start of the trail, Kinneret bent to look at a footprint. It was small, the toes bare and rounded.

"This has to be the boy's. I think we should follow the path and see if we can find him."

Calev nodded, and after drinking some of the cold spring water—he tested it first, taking just a drop on his finger and finding no strange feel or taste to the liquid—they began the trek through a less dense area of the wood.

Beech trees rattled their leaves. Chipmunks scurried from the undergrowth. With the sun glowing green through the leaves and the scent of sweet pine in the air, it was almost beautiful. The beauty of the cursed forest took hold of

Kinneret's senses like poison. She moved slower instead of running. Her limbs grew heavy, and she longed to fall to the pine needles and forget the world.

"Kinneret." Calev took her by the shoulders. "Are you all right?"

She blinked to clear her head. "Yes. Fine. About the boy. I wonder how he survived in this place. Why haven't the tree men claimed him?"

Still watching her, Calev walked by her side. "Did Oron say how long the boy had been here?"

"No, but if the boy knows about Runnos, he has to have been hiding for a while, right?"

The path turned east and widened at a clearing. A hut of stone, sticks, and moss huddled beside a twisting pine that reached toward the sky. Under a simple, square window, a pine sapling grew from a wooden bucket. Thick ivy crawled up the hut's side and onto its roof, but the area around the shelter was clear and nicely cared for. Someone lived here and lived fairly well. Kinneret was still trying to understand how that could be true when the door opened and a boy who looked about eleven or twelve years old walked into the hazy, forest light.

"Greetings. I'm Miach." He smiled shyly, then turned as a tiny goat trotted around his feet. "And this is Ethus."

Miach's innocent beauty struck Kinneret as hard as the forest's strange charm. His skin was so clean and young that it nearly seemed luminescent. He was thin, but looked well enough. She had an overwhelming urge to pick him up like she used to do with Avi.

Kinneret traded a look with Calev, who stepped forward.

"Miach, can we come inside and talk to you about this forest?" Calev asked.

The boy patted the goat's head and said quietly, "Yes." His words sounded furry or disjointed...wrong somehow. Like they began in another language and grew into something Kinneret could understand. "Come in. Stay awhile."

Calev shivered beside Kinneret. "I'm not sure about this."

"Me either. But how could a little boy be a danger?"

The inside of the hut showed the same kind of tidiness as the outside. The packed earth floor had been swept as clean as was possible for dirt. A small hearth in the far wall held a seasoned log, but no buildup of ashes. Small piles of acorns and berries lined the two shelves near the window and a small bed of moss and leaves sat in the corner.

Miach sat beside the hearth, pulled his knees up under his long tunic, and cuddled the goat under one arm.

"Did you call for help yesterday?" Calev knelt beside the boy.

Kinneret watched out the window, fully expecting a tree creature to come crashing down on them at any moment.

"I did. That's my job. I'm the lure."

Oh. Kinneret did not like the sound of that.

Calev froze in the act of scratching the baby goat's chin. "What is a lure?"

Kinneret tugged on Calev's sleeve. "We don't have sun to chat. Sorry. Time to go."

But Calev held back.

Miach stood, tears glistening in his big eyes. "I don't like it, but Runnos says it's the only way I can stay alive. He keeps my Ethus alive too. I have a debt to pay, Runnos says. My father was the blacksmith."

"We can help you escape," Kinneret said. "Tell us everything, and we'll come up with a plan."

She saw the moment Miach noticed the bark-like skin that

had crept up her fingers over the last few hours as well as the pine needles sprouting from her wrist. He tensed, then seemed to absorb the information like he'd seen this happen. Like it was no surprise. The urge to question him about what might be happening to her pushed at the back of her throat, but she shoved it down. First, they needed to get him talking about himself. They needed to know what they were dealing with.

"Please, Miach," she said. "Tell us how you ended up here."

The boy crossed his legs, and the tiny goat crawled into his lap. "I'd like to tell my story. I haven't told anyone in..." He looked out the window, dazed.

"When did you come to the forest?" Calev asked gently.

Miach blinked. "My father made a sword. Our village was strong with magic. He etched symbols of power and control into the weapon and the Silvanian king offered to buy it. Father said we wouldn't have to eat only bone marrow during the dry days anymore. He said we'd have enough silver to buy chickens. I love eggs."

"He has to be talking about Dante's sword." Kinneret gripped Calev's sleeve.

"But that weapon looks brand new. There isn't a sign of exposure anywhere on it. And Miach has obviously been here for...how long have you been here, Miach?" Calev scratched the goat again and it bleated sweetly.

"I don't know. We don't get old."

Kinneret traded yet another loaded look with Calev. This child was mad. He made no sense. If he couldn't even remember his age or how he came to be here, how was he going to help them resist Runnos and save Oron? "How old are you?"

"I used to be ten years old. Now I'm still ten years old."

A chill slithered down Kinneret's arms. "Still."

Miach met her gaze. "Still."

"Kinneret." Calev's voice was low and wary.

"Do you know the name of the Silvanian king?" Kinneret balled her skirt in her sweating hands.

"It's a funny name. I had an uncle with that name. Alfonso the Second."

Calev stood very slowly.

Kinneret took hold of his fingers.

"You must be mistaken, Miach." She smiled but she felt like vomiting. "Alfonso ruled one thousand years ago."

"Yes. That's it!" Miach hopped up, the goat with him, and started toward the shelves. "Would you like some berries before you die? They are very good for a last meal."

All right. Enough. "Calev, grab the goat." Kinneret gathered the boy up and hurried out of the door, ignoring his protests.

"Kin?" Calev's eyes went wide.

Kinneret looked over her shoulder. "We're getting out of here."

The sun slipped behind clouds above the forest as they headed back down the fern-lined path. Miach punched at Kinneret's back. He was surprisingly strong for a one thousand and ten-year-old.

"Stop that. We're going to help you escape this cursed forest. Whether you like it or not. You've been cursed yourself so you don't know what's good for you."

"I can't. I can't! He'll kill Ethus!"

"He won't. Calev has him. And Calev is from Old Farm, a place where animals are practically revered."

"Not exactly," Calev said. In other circumstances, she would've thought his adherence to absolute truth was adorable, but in this case...

"Yeah. Yeah. You treat them seas better than the rest of the world anyway."

"True, but...where are we going and what are we doing?" Calev asked.

"You're turning into one of them." Miach's little fists pounded against Kinneret's shoulder bone. "You've already lost. Just let me keep Ethus alive!"

Kinneret forced herself to speak calmly. "We're going to take Miach and Ethus back to Ona, Dante, and Oron, then figure out a plan to break out of this wood," she said in answer to Calev's question. "Everything is going to be fine. We might use your father's sword, Miach. He was a fine craftsman, wasn't he?"

Miach was crying a little, but at least he'd stopped with the punching. "Yes." His words still sounded odd, like someone was translating them inside Kinneret's head. She didn't like it one bit. "He also made a shield, but it's even more lost than the sword."

"A shield?" Calev trotted up beside them, the tiny goat in his arms. The creature seemed perfectly happy to be carried. It closed its little eyes and almost seemed to smile. "The sword has runes. Magic runes. Does the shield?"

Miach lifted himself a little to look at Calev. "Of course."

"Of course it does, Calev." Kinneret helped Miach move to a more comfortable position on her back. He'd stopped fighting her for now, but she wasn't about to let him down so he could run off and tell his friend Runnos all about them. "If the sword can kill green men, what can the shield do?"

"Protect a human from Runnos's commands. From his voice and—"

They passed under the branches of a spindly pine and an array of deep green needles brushed Kinneret, then Miach.

The boy went silent and very still.

Kinneret stopped and maneuvered Miach around so his belly was near hers and she faced him. "What is it, Miach?"

His eyes glazed and his lips parted.

Calev put the little goat between Miach and Kinneret. "Here is your friend. Talk to Ethus. Are you all right, Miach?"

Miach didn't seem to notice Ethus at all. "Runnos calls for my silence in this. I must be silent. He calls for your death." The boy's head spun to face Calev and the unnaturally quick movement made Kinneret feel sick. Miach looked to Kinneret then. "And you are chosen."

Then Miach's eyes fluttered shut and he fell against Ethus and Kinneret.

Before she could utter a question, a vibration buzzed through her fingers, the fingers gripping Miach's bare little legs.

Her view of him and his goat went black.

"Calev?" she called out, still feeling Miach and Ethus in her arms, but unable to see anything.

She couldn't hear Calev's answer or feel anything except her flesh contact with the boy and his pet through her altered fingertips.

Then the black lightened to gray. Shapes grew. Light filtered into view.

A group of men and women wearing long shirts in shades of ruby, vermillion, sage, and sunlight gathered around a sparkling waterfall. The water fell from a cliff well above their heads and kept on falling into the earth, a distance Kinneret couldn't quite make out. The spray cooled her face as she studied these people. They were dressed unlike anyone she'd ever seen. Ankle length cloaks clasped with intricate pins partially hid their loose, multi-colored pants. Bushy-haired children threaded back and forth through their elders.

The children were dressed like Miach.

He wore the same odd necklace and simple tunic like the other young ones. Though they spoke to one another and sought attention by pulling on their parents, they were too quiet for children. Something was wrong.

Kinneret looked down at herself and saw Miach's body.

She was Miach.

This had to be a memory.

Shuddering at the strangeness of it all, Kinneret walked toward a tall man, the one closest to the waterfall. His dark beard was wet from the spray.

Father, her mind said.

The wind kicked up and leaves blew hard against the group, twigs too. The ground rumbled with thunder.

"The forest god knows," Miach's father said, voice strong but strained.

He was obviously their chieftain. A weapons-maker as chief. That told Kinneret how ancient this memory was. Now, chiefs, kings, and kyros were politicians and warriors. Never craftsmen. But long ago, things were different.

"We must hide this shield," he said. "Then we'll find another place for the sword. We can go to the king, tell him the tale, and he can use his mighty forces to retrieve the objects. I won't let my family die for this."

Murmurs of agreement flowed through the group, then they hurried around the back of the waterfall. Kinneret followed, feet slipping slightly on the rocky path behind the sheet of water.

Miach's father waved the group on. "The green men will not

pass into this space." He held out a hand to Kinneret. "They hate strong water."

Kinneret's—Miach's—foot shot out from under her and she slid toward the ledge. Miach's father neatly grabbed her up and steadied her on the ground. A woman with long, thin braids walked up and put a gentle hand on Miach's shoulder. *Mother.*

"Be brave, my fine boy," she said.

Miach's father led the group into a damp cave behind the waterfall. Several men and women clapped their hands together and said a word that couldn't untangle itself in her mind. Light sprang to life between their fingers.

What magic they had! Where had this power gone over the centuries? Kinneret wondered if this was how it was in the Northern Isles where magic was still very strong.

The cave's pathway tightened to a space just wide enough for a child. The wet walls housed many-legged creatures Miach didn't want to touch. Kinneret wondered where Ethus was. He could've comforted Miach. But there didn't seem to be anything in his thoughts about the baby goat.

Miach's father rubbed his beard, then reached his glowing fingers through a small opening to survey what was on the other side of the cave wall. He leaned back out again and studied Miach. "Son. Are you brave enough to take this shield and tuck it away to save us all?"

The boy's trepidation echoed through Kinneret like a snake's rattle. "Yes, Father."

The man removed a round shield from his back and set it against a rock. "Solid ground lies past this opening. Set the shield there, then climb back out. I doubt the tree spirits will ever manage to find it."

Five bronze circles decorated the shield and each of the

shapes showed runes similar to the ones on the sword Dante found. Fitted leather edged the shape and regularly spaced dents in the metal between the circles showed off the tribe's craftsmanship. Stones had been set into the shield too, inside each of the bronze circles. One was a pearly white, another almost transparent—three more of differing colors winked in the torchlight.

Kinneret put her hand to her head, the scent of cave mud and fresh water in her nose. Miach's nose.

This was so disorienting.

Miach's father lifted him and set him on the rock outside the small opening that led deeper into the hill. Then the man handed the shield over. It was heavier than Kinneret had expected. Maybe it was because she only had a young boy's strength instead of her own at the moment. She wedged the shield through the oval of darkness, keeping one hand on the smooth, leather strap.

"Don't let it fall now." Their leader gently patted Miach's back with his illuminated hand.

"I won't, Father."

Kinneret moved her feet so they hung on the other side of the opening, then slid to the ground. Darkness blanketed the area, heavy and flat. Using only touch, Kinneret settled the shield on the cave floor, then turned to feel her way out. Strong hands helped her return to the family and the woman—*Mother* —cocooned Kinneret in her wiry arms.

They headed out of the cave, beyond the splashing waterfall, only to meet nine great tree men.

Scooping Kinneret up, Mother turned to run back into the cave to safety, but a vine, thick as a spear shaft, curled around her neck and yanked her to the ground. Kinneret was torn from her arms. Her heart sputtered like a dying candle as she watched a green man pull Mother into its trunk, where she disappeared.

Gone. Forever.

"Mother!" Tears tore down Kinneret's cheeks and she fell to her knees.

Father raised the rune-etched sword to slice off that same tree spirit's largest limb. The creature roared and grabbed the weapon. Hissing, it dropped the steel. The sword hit the ground beside Father who'd been knocked to his back. Father reached for the sword, but the green man's roots crawled over his middle and squeezed him until Kinneret had to turn away. Vomit burned her throat, mouth, and lips.

"Mother! Father!"

Then all the horror and fear crashed over Kinneret and the pine needled forest floor rose to meet her.

The world disappeared.

Darkness swamped her.

Kinneret woke to the feel of a gentle nudge to the head. She opened her eyes. Ethus wore a tiny goat smile. The small animal climbed onto Kinneret's chest and nestled its chin under hers. Love washed the desperate fear away. Dizzy, Kinneret saw two images lying on top of one another. Ethus on Miach's chest and Ethus on her own chest. She blinked and finally she was in her own body only instead of Miach's memory.

She sat up, dislodging Ethus as gently as she could in her state. Miach was now in Calev's arms. They knelt beside her.

"I saw his memory," she said to Calev, her voice rough with emotions she was never meant to feel. "Miach's memory."

"What did you see?"

"The shield. Miach put it in a cave. Behind a waterfall. His father was the chief and they died and…"

She was shaking and couldn't stop. Calev and Miach put arms around her. She closed her eyes and let them hold her. Ethus nibbled her left thumb and bleated loudly as if he wanted to tell her something.

Finally, they started in the direction of the grove. Miach wasn't fighting it, but Kinneret kept one hand latched to his tunic just in case he decided to run. She felt so differently about the boy now. She knew his pain. She'd felt it.

"I'm sorry about your family," she said, her words tiptoeing out of her mouth. She didn't want to wake the grief in him.

He held up her greening fingers. "You saw through these." His big eyes were such a frightening mix of cunning and innocence, if such a combination could exist. "Runnos and his green men can watch your life."

A shiver ran through Kinneret. She couldn't question him about the shield. Not yet. She had to let that experience wash over her first. Miach stumbled on the path and yawned widely. Maybe what she'd accidentally done to him had drained his strength. He stopped, eyes dropping shut.

Kinneret helped Calev gather up Miach. She tucked the baby goat under one arm gently. The animal bleated softly, but Miach made no sound aside from deep breathing.

Kinneret shook her head. "I don't like any of this. We obviously need to find that shield. But if Miach can't tell us where the waterfall is, it might take ages to find. And what does Runnos want with me? Miach said I'm becoming one of them. I'm assuming he doesn't simply mean I'm becoming a Silvanian," she said wryly. "I'm growing into a green man."

Calev's throat moved in a swallow. He wouldn't meet her

eyes and she knew it was because he was hiding unshed tears. "I won't let that happen. We won't let that happen."

The path gave way to the darker area of the wood where fog tangled in the undergrowth despite the sun that tried very hard to pierce the thick leaves overhead.

Kinneret held up a hand and splayed her fingers. They felt stronger. Like she could steer a boat in the worst of storms without breaking a sweat. But her fingers didn't look like hers anymore. They were someone else's. Some*thing* else's. An itch like she had some horrible disease spread over her neck and down her arms. She scratched at the bark growing along her ring finger and thumb until the altered flesh burned and bled.

Calev was suddenly close. "Stop that. It won't help." Keeping the sleeping Miach close to his chest, he reached out his own hand and cupped hers. His eyes were fierce and dark and she loved him so much. "I am here with you. I will not give up on you. We will win this. No matter what. We will get back to Avi. We will sail Ekrem's ship. You are Kaptan Kinneret and nothing is going to stop you."

Emotion surged through her chest and made her heart beat too quickly. She gripped his fingers hard. "I know. We will."

She kissed him like a promise made and they traveled deeper into the darkness.

13

ONA

"I wish I could get my head on straight."

Ona tried to separate herself from the pain of her two wounds so she could think. While Dante sipped watered wine from his flask and searched the grove for edible plants, she took three breaths. Her injured ribs didn't want her to breathe deeply, but she did her best. Oron had been quiet for the last hour, so she kept her voice down.

"When Lucca and I raided an enemy's stronghold, we always sent at least two of our party into the heart of the set up. In the war room, or the keep, or the master's bedroom if it was late at night. We need to find this forest's heart and strike there to win." She realized Dante was staring, open-mouthed. "What?"

"You don't sound unsure of yourself right now. You sound every bit like a mercenary."

He wasn't wrong. Maybe strategy was removed enough from the actual violence that her broken mind could handle it. "Well, let's enjoy it while we can, hmm? Who knows when I'll become a mess of tears and snot again?" She rolled her eyes at herself.

Dante handed her some dark, black berries. "They're safe. See?" He popped two between his lips and Ona tried not to gape.

"I'm going to wait and see if you die."

"Good idea." Dante chewed and stared up into the canopy. The tendons in his neck stood out. He had a tiny birthmark under his left ear.

"It looks like an arrowhead."

"What?"

"Your birthmark. It has the shape of an arrowhead."

He put a hand over it, then let his fingers slide away. "Lucca thought it was an *older brother mark* when he was little. He said all older brothers had them." Dante chuckled. "He thought he knew everything."

Anger flared inside Ona, sudden and unexpected. "Weren't you worried about him when you left? What if your father had decided to beat Lucca in your absence? And what about your mother?"

Dante had the decency to look ashamed. "I was a child. Thirteen years of age. In my mind, my father hated only me. The family didn't function because of me. I thought leaving would make everything better for them all."

Ona's anger cooled. She remembered feeling like that as a child. Like every problem centered on her. Dante had been too young to understand that his father was the problem and he himself was not at fault.

She touched his hand and gave him a sad smile. "But you know better now."

"I still wish I hadn't left them."

"It does no good to beat yourself up about it. It was an awful situation. You did what you thought was right."

"Maybe you need to say some of those things to yourself."

Ona shut her feelings off. They'd talked enough. Now was the time to plan.

"Back to our strategy. Where could the heart of this forest be?" Ignoring the pain, she stood and walked around the grove. "This could be it. That fog and the animals and Oron here...this seems like an active place."

"True. But you'd think Runnos would be present in the heart of his sacred wood. If he only speaks here occasionally, I don't think this is it."

"I disagree. He might be wise enough to keep his most vulnerable spot hidden."

"He might not have a vulnerable spot."

"Everyone has a weakness. Something they hold highest and would die without." For her, it had been avenging her aunt. Now, it was somehow, some way, to reunite with Lucca. Lucca and Seren were her priority, her heart—her weakness and her strength in one.

"I don't." Dante's voice cut through her thoughts. He pressed the tip of his blade against his palm, not hard enough to draw blood, but just to pinch the skin.

"At the least, you care about not feeling pain."

He cocked his head, then nodded. "Yes. I guess you're right. That's pretty sad though. I only care about my own well-being. I need some new priorities."

His gaze locked with hers. A strange heat flooded Ona's body. He held the sword at an angle, the tip digging lightly into the forest floor. He'd tied his hair back and his cheekbones stood out. She remembered exactly how gentle his hands had been during their journey with the Invaders.

She turned away, swallowing. "I think my wound is healing. Kinneret's abilities are better than she guessed."

"I'm glad." Dante went to Oron's tree and spoke into the opening. "Sailor, sorry to wake you, but would you like some watered wine?"

Oron grunted. "If you can manage it, that would be good."

Dante did as Kinneret had earlier, wetting the end of a cloth he had stored in a small bag on his belt.

Oron sputtered. "Wait. I hear them. I caught something in their whispers."

Dante pulled the cloth away.

Oron said something else, but Ona couldn't catch it. She scrambled up the side of the tree, leaning in as close as possible to Oron's face. But she still couldn't hear his strangled words.

"Let me help." Dante lifted Ona with one arm and she braced herself against the rough pine bark. Pine sap permeated the air and stuck between Ona's fingers.

"Oron. Say it one more time. Please. If you can," she touched his head lightly, the half-broken trunk scratching her skin and making it ooze blood.

"I heard them. The sword."

"Yes." Dante, eyes fierce, held up the weapon so Oron could glimpse it. "We have it, sailor. Is there something you think we should do with it specifically?"

"No. There is also a shield. The smithy made a shield too. If you have both—"

Coughing broke off his sentence.

"Oron!" Ona's heart pinched at the sight of tears streaming from the brave man's one visible eye.

Dante held the dampened cloth to Ona. "Try giving him a drink."

She took the cloth, but Oron's eye had closed. He breathed shallowly like someone very sick and nearing death. She shook her head at Dante. He lowered her down, then tucked the cloth away.

"Did I hear him mention a shield?" Dante sheathed the sword in his belt.

"He said the blacksmith who crafted the sword also made a shield to go with it. If the sword is the only weapon the green men truly fear, then what might the shield do?"

Dante linked his fingers behind his neck and breathed out, his gaze going from Oron's tree to the ground. Circles were beginning to color the soft skin below his light eyes. Old Ona would've demanded that he snap out of his fatigue and fight on, but new Ona considered things differently.

"Why don't you sleep for a while? I'll keep watch. Give me the sword and rest. Then we can think together."

Dante looked reluctant, but he gave the weapon over. "Are you certain you feel strong enough?" He eyed her wounded side and shoulder.

"I am. I promise. Just for a little bit. Pushing through fatigue is stupid and I'm done with being stupid when I can help it."

The corner of his handsome lips lifted, and he lay flat at the base of Oron's tree, hands resting on his flat stomach.

He was asleep in five heartbeats. He was definitely a soldier. Warriors could sleep at will. Ona knew the feeling well.

"Get those dreams while you can, warrior," she whispered, standing guard over him. "This is for Lucca. And also, a little bit, for you."

She couldn't help but enjoy the look of Dante's sleeping

form. She could almost see the thirteen year old boy in him, the one who had run away in hopes of fixing everything in his broken home.

Raising the sword and clearing her wistful thoughts away, she waited for the attack that would surely come. It had been far too long since a tree creature made an appearance.

14

KINNERET

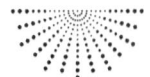

Kinneret and Calev crashed into the grove with Miach and Ethus, surprising a sword-wielding Ona and a sleeping Dante. Ona looked ready to pass out. Probably from her many injuries. She was a tough one, that was for sure.

"How is Oron?" Kinneret went immediately to the tree. The trunk had grown. Now she could only touch half his head of hair rather than the whole expanse. "Oron?"

A hand touched Kinneret's arm. It was Ona. "He has been… asleep for a while," Ona said.

"I will get you out of there, friend," Kinneret whispered.

Then she filled Ona and Dante in on how she'd accessed Miach's memory and the way Runnos seemed to stop the boy from telling them about the shield.

"Runnos did the same thing to Oron," Ona said.

"So is this the boy who called for us?" Dante took Miach

from Calev and set him carefully on a patch of mossy growth in the center of the grove.

"What is the story with the goat?" Ona cocked an eyebrow and bent to pet the goat gently. Kinneret thought maybe she was about to cry. The woman wiped her eye with the back of a hand roughly, then stood. Why would the sight of a goat make her want to weep?

Kinneret gave Oron's head one more touch. Her heart weighed a ton. They had to get Oron out of there. "Ethus is Miach's friend. They are immortal."

Calev picked up where she left off. "Runnos gave the boy and his pet eternal life in exchange for luring prey to the wood."

Dante shook his head, disgusted.

Ona kicked a tree root, then sat down, cross-legged, beside the boy. She took his little hand in hers. Kinneret wondered what she was searching for in those fingers. Evidence that he was a working part of the cursed forest?

"He isn't the only one falling into Runnos's plans." Kinneret showed her own hands. They were so much worse and her feet were feeling strange too. Eyeing her sandals, a sweat broke over her forehead. Her toes seemed to be melding into one and were oddly flexible. Her stomach turned. "I think I'm becoming a green man, as you call them." Ona's eyes were pitying and Kinneret loathed the look. "I'll fight it. I'll be fine. What did Oron say before Runnos put him to sleep?"

A branch snapped beyond the grove.

Dante was standing, runed sword poised, before Kinneret could move an inch. They all stayed still, listening. A crow called, and they all jumped a little.

Dante glanced at Kinneret. "Oron told us there is a shield

that was made alongside this sword. It seemed like he thought if we had both, we'd stand a better chance of surviving this."

"That goes along with what Miach said before Runnos stopped his tongue."

Calev ran a hand over the boy's head. "Can you tell us where the shield is, Miach?"

Miach's eyes fluttered open. He looked like himself again, the foggy look gone. He reached for Ethus and the goat snuggled up beside him.

"I can't tell you. Runnos will take our lives away. He won't let me tell you even if I wanted to. His power...it's in my mouth. I can feel it." He moved his tongue and crinkled his immortal nose.

Kinneret punched her thigh, frustrated.

Dante came up beside her. "Couldn't you simply go into the boy's memory again? Maybe you'd spot some area details that would help us locate the waterfall and the cave."

"It wasn't simple. Miach blacked out after I did that. We need to let him rest. Just for a short time. Don't we?"

Ona shrugged. "I really don't know."

"He's immortal, right? It's not going to kill him," Dante said. "And staying here with Runnos and his henchmen might be the end of the rest of us."

"He makes a good case," Calev said. "If we are injured or killed, Miach and Ethus won't have anyone to help them escape."

"We're not escaping," Miach said. "I've told you. Eat some good berries. Death comes." Miach didn't look at them. He scratched Ethus's ears and set his cheek on the goat's bumpy little back. "It's better if you don't think about it."

Kinneret and the rest of the adults swapped horrified glances. This little boy definitely needed their help whether he knew it or not. "Let's take some sun to rest and eat those greens and berries you've gathered there, Dante."

Dante doled out handfuls of edibles as the group arranged themselves in a circle, backs to the center where Miach and Ethus settled down for a nap.

"I'll keep first watch." With Dante's sword, Ona began a slow circuit around the grove. "Your healing worked wonders, Kinneret. Thank you. I won't hesitate to defend you this time. I swear it. But maybe someone should join me."

Kinneret could tell that admission cost Ona quite a bit. "I'll join you," she said, taking her dagger from her sash. "Sleep, Dante and Calev. We'll need you soon."

Both men nodded and lay on their sides.

The sun through the trees dimmed and turned greener as the afternoon faded into evening. Watching the trees, Kinneret and Ona shared stories about friends and family, treasure and victories, and their best days.

Kinneret's smile faded. "What is one thing you would change if you could move the sun back?"

Ona switched her grip on the magic-infused sword and didn't meet Kinneret's eyes. "I would side with Seren, not her enemy. I can't even imagine what she and Lucca think of me now. Well, they think I'm dead, but I guarantee they're cursing my ghost."

"I doubt it. You surely had some good reason for going against them. You were all fighting the same larger threat. The Invaders. Right?"

"Yes, but the reason I sided against Seren and Lucca was to win. Defeating the Invaders and killing as many of them as I could, that was my only focus. I let that thirst for revenge ruin the one thing I still had. Lucca will never forgive me. But I'm going to ask anyway. It's the least I can do. That and reunite him with his brother."

"That'll score you some points, surely." Kinneret nudged Ona with an elbow, trying to cheer her. "It won't hurt that Dante thinks you're amazing. He'll speak well of you to them. Of how you've changed."

Ona's head whipped around to look at Dante. "He doesn't think I'm amazing."

Dante snorted and rolled over, snoozing soundly despite being in the middle of a forest of monsters. Kinneret longed for his brand of courage. Or was it stupidity? Well, she wanted whatever made that enviable sleep possible.

"Yes, he does," Kinneret said. "He watches your every move and can't keep the admiration out of those blue eyes of his."

"They're actually more of a steel color. And his—" Ona's mouth hung open as she realized Kinneret was smirking. "Oh shut up. Fine. We might be fond of one another. It's just because of our shared love of Lucca."

"Sure."

A low growl rumbled from the south side of the forest.

Kinneret whirled around only to come face-to-face with a tangle of red-tinged ivy.

She thrashed at the vines as they spun around her ankle. The dagger had little effect, but Ona was behind her in a flash. She drove the runed sword down, slicing the ivy in a clean strike as the men woke.

"Get Miach." Kinneret ignored the fact that the ivy didn't burn her skin like it had the first time she'd been wrapped in its red-green leaves.

Calev grabbed the boy, who remained unnaturally asleep.

Dante took the sword from Ona, who was sweating like she was fevered. She obviously couldn't fight for long with the injuries suffered by both her body and her mind.

They braced for another attack, but the ivy slithered back into the sun-dappled forest.

"Oron?" Kinneret hoped he was still alive. She couldn't bear to think of losing him. So far, she'd refused to let her mind even consider that outcome. "Oron?"

Running to the half-broken tree that held him, she peered inside. The tree now grew over his entire head and both shoulders. Only one spot of his jawline was visible. Chest tight, she pressed her knuckle against the skin there. Oron had been there for her ever since she lost her parents. He was the reason they won over the oramiral at Quarry Isle. He won over the slaves there. He was the reason she'd never truly felt abandoned when death took her parents. Forcing her tears back, she turned to face Ona, Calev, and Dante.

"He's dying. We can't stay here and rest anymore. And guarding him is doing nothing. Runnos is still taking him."

Calev pressed his hand against the tree and whispered Oron's name along with an Old Farm prayer.

"We have to find that shield," Kinneret said, "and figure out how to use both of Miach's family heirlooms to destroy Runnos. That is the only way we can save him and escape this cursed forest."

"All right." Dante sheathed the sword and spread his hands wide. "Since there is a spring northeast of here, near Miach's hut, like you mentioned, then there may be a convergence of water, leading to a creek, which could produce a waterfall south of here."

Kinneret squeezed her eyes shut to recall what she had seen in Miach's memory. "The waterfall dropped into a deep crevasse. Anyone know of a fault line near here? A place where the earth shakes sometimes?" She'd heard of such things from Oron, who'd traveled all over the world as a trader before working for her.

"Oh yes!" Ona pointed excitedly to the South. "I've never been there, but my aunt used to talk about a town that was eaten up by the earth before Silvania was even a country. All that was left of the town was a great scar in the ground."

"Outside the wood?" Calev handed Miach off to Kinneret, who'd tucked her dagger away.

She hated how her tree-like fingers looked against his skin and hoped she wouldn't be thrown into any of his memories again. She'd hate to hurt him. "Are you sure I should hold him? I might do that thing again."

"If you do, we'll know more."

Ona nodded. "He is immortal."

Kinneret swallowed and held the boy carefully.

"Is the crevasse outside the wood then?" Dante asked. "Will we even be able to access it? Runnos might not let us out."

Kinneret started southward. "We won't know until we try."

THE FOREST DARKENED as Kinneret led them through more pine groves, oaks with trunks wide as her old boat, and paths riddled with mossy roots and thick ferns. Branches cracked in the distance every once in a while, putting them all on alert. Dante kept his sword poised and Calev had his dagger ready. Ona's gaze watched movement that Kinneret couldn't even see.

Kinneret's sandals rubbed her changing skin and she finally had to stop.

Miach woke and went right to Ona like he knew her. Ethus had been circling Ona's ankles since the sun began to set. "Where are we?" he asked Ona.

Kinneret sat and tore off her sandals. Her stomach rolled. She tried not to look at her feet. They felt very wrong and staring at them wouldn't fix anything.

"We're headed to the waterfall to get the shield," Ona answered, her gaze on Kinneret's ripped up shoes.

Miach went pale. "We can't. He'll find out. Runnos will kill Ethus." He grabbed the baby goat and held it tightly.

Calev put a hand on Miach's shoulder. "We won't let that happen. I'm good luck."

"He is." Kinneret managed a smile as they started forward again. "I'd be dead long ago if it weren't for his good luck."

"See? We'll be just fine." In the gathering dark, Calev graced the boy with his best smile.

Ona came close. "Good luck? I thought that was all your salt magic? That's the way everyone tells the story anyway."

Kinneret waved her off. "Without his luck, I wouldn't have had a chance to use it."

"Really."

Kinneret nodded.

Dante clapped Calev on the back. "I don't pretend that bad luck was the reason my life has been the horror it's been. That's all me and my bull-headedness. But I'd love to think some of your good luck might find its way to me."

Calev smiled even as he kept an eye on the trees hulking over the animal trail they walked. He took a shamar yam shell from his sash and handed it over to the wide-shouldered,

former Invader. "Take this. Say a prayer into it and you may find more than luck. You might find faith."

Dante took the purple-striped shell and kissed it. "I'll do that. Faith is something I've never found, but I wish for it every day."

Calev laughed. "That *is* faith, Silvanian. If you didn't believe it was going to happen, you wouldn't continually wish for it."

Pocketing the shell, Dante blinked. "I never thought of it like that."

Kinneret's own laugh was cut off when Runnos began speaking inside her head.

She jerked to a stop and Ona smashed into her back.

Come to me. Come to me. Come. To. Me.

The words were like hands, warm and smooth, gliding through her hair and down the back of her neck. Her breath left her and goosebumps rose along her arms.

We will be one. My power is your power. My darkness is your darkness, strong one. Come. To. Me.

The path faded into a dull green. The trees around her glowed a deep blue-green. She whirled and saw a flame of orange and red in the shape of Ona.

"Kinneret?" Ona's voice warbled like she was underwater.

Another flame came close. This one touched Kinneret, and her flesh ignited with a fierce need. A hunger.

This was so wrong.

She screamed.

The world returned.

There was Calev standing in front of her, eyes full of worry, his hand on her arm. Ona, Dante, Miach, and the little goat circled her.

"Runnos took my mind..." Her head pounded like his voice

knocked on the door of her thoughts. "No." She gripped her head, branching fingers digging into her scalp. "Go away!"

The pulsing echo of Runnos's power disappeared.

Calev took her in his arms. "You fought him off, didn't you? See? You're going to beat him at his game. You are far too strong for him. You are Kinneret Raza, salt witch, full-ship kaptan to an amir, and the best sailor the world has ever seen."

She sucked a breath and swallowed. "I saw you as a pillar of fire. Ona too."

Ona grimaced. "You looked like you enjoyed it a little bit. I hate to say it, but maybe you should be aware of that."

"No, you're right. I did." Kinneret's cheeks heated. "Runnos is disgustingly tempting. It's awful."

Dante held out the hilt of the magic sword. "I wonder what would happen if you tried to hold this? Maybe it would drive that god out of your flesh."

It wasn't a horrible idea. She took the sword.

The moment her hand curled around the hilt, her entire being caught fire. At least, that was how she felt. The pain roared in her aching head and she threw the weapon with surprising force across the path and into a clutch of ferns.

"Well, that didn't work." Ona went to fetch the runed steel.

Calev crossed his arms. "Understatement."

The night weighed down Kinneret's shoulders. With every step closer to the edge of the forest, with every snap of a branch in the distance, with every whisper from Runnos, she sank deeper and deeper into a mood that fit the darkness. She was almost certain the god wouldn't let her leave the forest's boundary line. How she knew that, well, she wasn't sure. That would mean the rest of them would go on to search for the waterfall and the cave without her. She'd be left to Runnos. Left to his temptation. And she didn't know whether she could shake him off again so easily. Someone could stay with her, she supposed, but then they'd be at risk if she lost her mind. Who knew what she'd do? She couldn't ask someone to risk that.

She'd have to grit her teeth and hold on and fight the god herself.

15

KINNERET

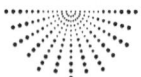

Thick trees blocked any trace of moonlight. Only a faint glow in the distance showed where the forest ended and the sky showed itself. Darkness had always made Kinneret's hands sweat. After all, at sea she rarely experienced full dark. Even intense cloud cover let a haze of moonlight through somewhere over the water and the waves reflected it. But now, with the dense leaves and what must've been a cloud bank over this forest, there was no light except for that distant goal—the end of the wood.

Suddenly, pricks of pain stopped her.

"Halt." Dante's voice called out to her left. "I think we've wandered into a patch of thorns."

Everyone was making noises of discomfort around her.

"Well, let's back up." She gripped the thorns crowding her feet and legs, enduring the burn of their sharp ends to yank them away.

"Don't pull on them," Calev said.

Before she could ask why, the thorns crushed against her skirt, piercing the fabric to plunge into the flesh beneath. She howled in pain and surprise.

"When you fight them, they just grip more tightly," Calev said.

Ona grunted. "I'm trying my dagger." An owl's call covered the sound of her attempts. "It isn't working. It seems to grow back right away. Maybe the runed sword will make a dent."

"I'm giving it a go," Dante said through what sounded like gritted teeth. "I can't...I can't even lift the sword, let alone use it. They're everywhere."

Something flapped overhead and tossed Kinneret's hair. "I'm hoping that was a bat."

"What?" Miach asked, his voice trembling.

"Nothing. All right. I can get into my salt pouch. Maybe my magic will do something. Anything. Who knows?"

As she reached into her bag, a thorn dragged itself up her arm like a tiny knife. The pain was impressive considering the size of the thorn. With a pinch of salt held awkwardly in her fingers, she whispered.

"Blood of the sea,
Free me.
Hear my call,
Free us all."

The salt fell easily from her fingers. She held her breath.

Then the thorns pulled away from her.

"It worked! I can lift my arm. Hold on, I'll—"

The plant lunged at her, this time holding her closer and impaling her in one hundred different spots.

"Kinneret?" Ona's voice was gentle and wary.

"I was wrong. All the thorns came closer. It worked for a

125

moment like the plant was trying to decide if it accepted Salt Magic."

A crunching sound carried on the breeze.

"What is that noise?" Calev asked.

"Ethus is eating the thorns," Miach said. "I think he likes them."

"Sadly, I doubt that little fellow has enough stomach room to eat a way out for everyone," Dante said.

They all gasped as the plant tightened its grip.

"Help!" Miach sniffed and moaned pitifully, tugging at Kinneret's heart.

Calev cleared his throat. "I...I have an idea." He hissed in pain. "I'm thinking this is a darkthorn bush. It can take these plants ages to get this large. This is truly an elder and maybe it deserves some serious respect. Maybe even a sacrifice."

Dante snorted.

Kinneret glared at the warrior even though it was black as pitch and he'd never see it. "Listen to him."

"Aye, aye," Dante said.

The thorns squeezed Kinneret's waist and crept higher.

Calev coughed. "This won't feel wonderful, but repeat after me if you're up for trying my plan."

Ona called Miach's name. "Are you listening? Calev is a good man. Follow his directions and the pain will be over soon."

"All right, Ona," Miach whispered.

Thorns reached up Kinneret's back. Pinpricks of heat flayed her skin under her shirt.

"Elder," Calev said, "we respect you and offer our lifefluid to show our earnest apology for breaking into your land and crushing your growth beneath our feet. Everyone, grip the thorns in your less useful hand. Let the points prick you. Let the elder see we are genuine."

"This is ridiculous," Dante whispered.

"Just do it," Kinneret snapped.

They repeated Calev's words as best they could, stumbling over the phrasing here and there. Then Miach yelled as Kinneret gripped the plant in her left hand. Hot blood pooled around her fingers and the vicious spines of the darkthorn bush. She clenched her jaw and kept her hand in place, hoping it wasn't too terrible for the others, especially Miach.

Insects chirruped in the trees and more bats fluttered past.

Ona sighed raggedly. "I don't think—"

The thorns retreated with a dragging sound and Calev whooped in delight. Finally, Kinneret could move without jabbing pain. She hurried toward the light marking the end of the wood, grabbing whomever was closest. "Let's get out of here before that plant decides it wants a finger or two."

"Agreed!" Calev took her arm.

"Nice work back there," she said.

"At your service, Kaptan."

Dante's deep voice called Calev. "Apologies for my continued lack of faith, Old Farm. In the future, I will trust your instincts."

"Thank you." Calev stopped to clap Dante on the back. Kinneret could just barely make out their silhouettes.

"Enough sweet talk," Ona barked. "Like Kinneret, I'd rather not lose any body parts to this forest if I can help it."

THE FOREST abruptly stopped at a moonlit meadow dotted with boulders that looked like sleeping beasts.

The last time Kinneret had seen this place was in Miach's memory. And it had been colored in his family's blood.

Miach released Ona's hand and stood staring.

Kinneret touched his shoulder. "You honor them with your courage. With the way you show love to Ethus."

She heard him swallow. He nodded jerkily, then went back to clutching Ona's fingers. Dried blood showed on his wrist. He was one thousand and ten years old, but he seemed like any sweet, little child that had lost loved ones. From what Ona had told Kinneret during their watch, those two had a great deal in common.

She said a silent prayer for Oron, her own family that she was in danger of losing. Pressing a hand against her heart, she drew courage from the fierce need to save him.

Ona and Miach started toward the forest's last trees.

A new thought occurred to Kinneret. "Will Runnos allow you to go past the boundary, Miach?"

"Yes." His voice was small and shaky, his gaze on the field where he'd watched his kin fall to the green men. "I have a little distance I can walk before I get sick. That way, I can call out to travelers who don't come right up on the wood."

Calev's eyebrows knotted. He whispered something sharp under his breath about Runnos.

"Well, maybe I'll be able to go too," Kinneret said.

Calev cocked his head. "You didn't think you could?"

Kinneret shrugged, tears burning the corners of her eyes. She willed them away, then stepped into the meadow with her strange feet. "I feel the same. I can do this."

Dante started into the low grass, Ona behind him with Miach and Ethus. "We should hear a waterfall of that size if we get anywhere close."

"What if the waterfall isn't flowing anymore?" Ona asked. "Miach's family was here so long ago."

Kinneret walked beside Calev, grateful beyond words that she was able to stay beside him during this nightmare of an adventure. She was so glad Avi wasn't here. Her sister had been through enough. "There should still be a crevasse and a cave."

"True." Dante pointed. "There. See the line of paler ground? I'd bet all my silver that's it."

"You don't have any silver, do you?" Ona eyed him.

"Oh. No. I don't. And come to that, I don't have any more dried meat or bread either. Does anyone else have any food?"

They'd passed the fresh water from the spring that Calev and Kinneret had gathered in their waterskins, but no one had shared a bite of this or that in hours. Kinneret realized she wasn't even hungry. Not for meat or bread.

That strange darkness swarmed around her mind and she shook her head harshly to clear her thoughts. Calev put an arm around her shoulders and gave her a squeeze.

"I think we're out." Ona closed up the pouch on her belt and scrunched her mouth. "Dante, after we nab this shield, and if we live through it, do you think you can scrounge some more of those berries or leafy greens for us?"

He bowed his head. "I certainly will try."

Kinneret touched the puncture wounds the thorns had made on her hand. As they walked on, she wondered when Runnos would discover what they were up to and how much they would bleed when he did.

16

ONA

Half way between the supposed gigantic crack in the earth and the wood's boundary line, Ona paused, Dante coming up beside her. Miach still held her hand. A sudden thought had occurred to her and she wondered why she hadn't considered it earlier.

"Dante."

"Ona."

"Why aren't we escaping right now?" she whispered.

He rubbed his lip with a knuckle.

"I mean," she said, "Runnos doesn't seem to be sending any more green men out here. The old me would've already been gone. Well, I might've dragged you along for Lucca's sake and maybe for the pleasure of your handsome company, but I'm telling you, I would've been gone already. Why aren't we taking off?"

"You really were pretty terrible before your injury, weren't you?"

"I was."

"So answer it yourself, Onaratta. Why aren't you high tailing it out of this hell with me in tow already?"

Behind them, the line of pine trees swayed in the wind and the scent of night rose. Water, danger, animal scents. She shivered. "Because there is a man trapped in there. He'll probably die anyway, but we still have a chance to save him."

"And?"

"And Kinneret. We have to try to help her. She doesn't seem quite as innocent as some, but I like her. She made herself a legend in spite of ridiculous odds. Like Seren. I admire her."

"What about…" He jerked his chin toward Miach and Ethus.

Ona's throat tightened. "He is the enemy," she whispered in Dante's ear. "He is. If you think about it. He spies for Runnos, works for Runnos."

"You still want to save him." It wasn't a question and Dante was right.

"He lost them." Ona's aunt screamed in her memory, beat her hands against the Invaders. "I would never, ever leave him. I know how it feels to lose that much. In that way. I won't leave him. Or any of them."

"Then we're of the same mind."

Ona nodded, feeling oddly at ease. Her brush with death, her aunt's memory, and that last look at Lucca on the walls of Akhayma had smothered the flame of selfish, over-focused revenge. She didn't know what would drive her now. But doing her best to save these people—this was something she could latch on to.

Kinneret and Miach paused in unison. The boy's hand tugged at Ona's and he held his stomach. Ethus bumped his leg, then circled him three times.

Kinneret doubled over. Her skin was taking on an eerie greenish tone. What would happen if they couldn't stop her from changing? Would they be forced to cut her down with Dante's sword?

"You all right?" Ona asked Miach.

"We can keep going." He grimaced, then spoke to Kinneret, his partner in discomfort. "It will get a lot worse before we pass out."

Dante squatted beside Miach. "So you've tried to escape and Runnos knocked you out?"

"Yes."

Dante ruffled Miach's black hair. "Brave man."

A sad smile pulled at Ona's lips. She hoped with everything in her that she'd be able to reunite Dante with Lucca.

Miach grinned up at the large warrior. "Will I someday have muscles like yours?" The boy poked at Dante's impressive arm.

Dante looked at the ground for a breath. For all they knew, Miach would never grow up. He was stuck in this...strange suspended age of ten years. If they took down Runnos, he might die. Would he become a pile of one thousand and ten-year-old dust?

"Of course you will, boy. Of course you will." Dante stood and strode forward, shoulders bent and head tipped down.

Ona could see the cost that lie had reaped from Dante. He'd had to tell it though. Why scare the little fellow more than he already was? No point in that. Miach's father had doomed his son the moment he began crafting that sword and shield.

The moon rose high and bathed the meadow in light. The smoother areas looked much like the silver pool of magic water in the wood. What was the purpose of that strangely spelled body of water? Had it always been there? It was most likely

Runnos's doing, but it didn't seem to serve his needs very well. Surely the god could've done a little better than leaving the effects to chance. Wouldn't he want everyone who entered the pool to be turned into a green man to serve him or something like that? Why bother with blessing some people like he had Dante? And the water had healed Kinneret's boils at the same time that it began her transformation into a spirit of the wood. Why did the magic there seem at war with itself?

The group had been quiet since Dante's sad lie, and Ona didn't care to break it now with a question about a silver pool they'd hopefully never have to visit again. Miach might know about it though. She'd ask him later. Maybe she'd question him after they had the shield and were on the search for the sacred grove, for the heart of Runnos's home here in Silvania.

One more rise of ground, and the great crack in the earth appeared at their feet.

Ona stopped the stumbling Miach from going too close. Tufts of short grasses hung over the edge, and it was too dark to see how far down the break in the ground reached. The main stretch of the abyss ran roughly northeast toward the wood, but a long branch of it broke off here and wriggled north.

"But where's the waterfall?" Kinneret's voice was a croak. She and Miach were obviously feeling dizzy and sick.

"I suppose the flow of the waters did change. But look at that wall of rock there." Calev pointed beyond the chasm's northward trek to a dark patch in the moonlight. "That could very well be a cave."

"And we'll need to cross this death trap to get to it." Dante began searching behind boulders and in the few clumps of small trees. "We need a bridge. Or a vaulting pole."

Kinneret leaned against a jagged rock. A sparkling line of

white crystal spanned the front corner. Her pointed fingers curled around the crystal like vines around a tree branch. Ona fought a shiver.

"I'm not going to be leaping over anything right now," Kinneret said. "I doubt Miach is very excited about that either."

"I'll stay with you." Miach and Ethus joined Kinneret on the boulder. Ethus nibbled at Miach's tunic, and the boy gently nudged him away from the cloth. He picked some grass and fed the tiny animal from his outstretched palm.

Dante gripped a small tree's largest limb and yanked hard. Calev grabbed a hold to help.

"One, two, three!" Dante's arms bulged as he and Calev forced the branch down, snapping it away from the tree.

Ona bent to look into Miach's face. His eyes were as big as the moon above. He had to be remembering what happened in this place and the loved ones he'd lost in such a violent manner. She knew how that felt.

A sudden memory attacked her.

She saw her aunt laughing, sketching charcoal in hand. Two goats about Ethus's size stood on the table beside her paints. They'd tipped one jar over and blue ran down the table leg to puddle on the tiles.

Then the memory flashed forward and the Invaders were crashing into the room.

Her aunt lay on the tiled floor. Blood. Blood. Blood.

Breathing heavily, Ona realized Miach was shaking her arms. "Ona. Ona!"

"I'm fine. It was a long time ago." She breathed in slowly, trying to calm her frantic pulse. "They killed my aunt. She was my only family."

Miach drew her into a fierce hug. "I know. Shhh. I know."

He didn't know a thing about it, but here he was caring for her all the same in the best way he knew how.

She hugged him back, then drew away to look into those big eyes. "You do understand, don't you?"

He nodded, lips quivering and gaze darting around the meadow. His memories of this place still lived in his head and heart.

"We'll be strong together, all right?" Ona whispered.

"All right." He smiled and Ona felt something stir inside her.

Something that felt oddly like power. Like she was about to chant.

She pushed the feeling away. This was no time for violence. What was her body doing? Why had she thought of chanting at this moment?

"It's going to reach," Dante said.

He finished positioning the tree limb while Calev and Kinneret piled rocks on either side of the limb to keep it from rolling. When had Kinneret left the boulder? Ona's mind must've been truly gone for a moment. They tore three more limbs from the small trees near the crevasse and attempted to make a bridge.

After one last hug from Miach, Ona joined Dante. "This is not going to be fun."

Kinneret snorted and headed back to Miach. "No. But it won't be dull."

Calev's smile was there and gone in a blink. "That's my fire," he said quietly.

"I'll go first." Dante stepped onto the makeshift bridge.

The wood cracked ominously.

"Dante." Ona stepped closer. The scent of wet earth rose from the great crack in the ground. "Careful."

"I don't think any more of you should go across this." Eyes squinted in concentration, Dante paused about three-quarters from the other side. "I can get the shield."

"No, you can't." Miach shook his head. He tried to say more, but it looked as though his mouth wasn't working.

"He's right," Kinneret said. "I remember seeing the small hole Miach climbed through to hide the shield on the other side of the—"

Kinneret's face froze.

A gurgling sound came from her throat like she was choking. Calev ran to her and quickly untied his waterskin. He put the vessel to her lips, but she pushed it away, gasping.

"I'm not choking. Runnos just won't let us talk about...it." Kinneret did take a drink, then she kissed Calev's wrist.

Ona turned away to see how Dante was doing. His arms wheeled in a circle. He was only a step from the other side. Her heart hung limply in her chest. "Just jump it. Go on!"

He glanced at her, then flung himself toward the cave side of the chasm. Ona held her breath until his body rolled onto the earth, safe and whole, his hair and white teeth shining in the moonlight.

"I made it!" He brushed himself off and stood. "So I won't fit. All right. I'll hold the bridge from this side, and you, Ona, come on over with me. You're small and strong. You'll be able to fit I bet. Miach, what do you think?"

The boy nodded, lips white and pinched. Ethus bleated loudly in Dante's direction.

"Thanks for the affirmation, Sir Goat." Dante tipped his head to Ethus, then got onto his knees to support the bridge.

"Sir?" Kinneret looked to Calev like she didn't understand Dante's meaning.

"It's a label of respect. Of nobility," Calev said. "It doesn't translate well." He picked up one of the smaller branches they'd torn from the larger limb and began fashioning it into a torch.

Ona nodded at Calev's description. Thankfully, she and Dante spoke the trade tongue well enough to avoid too many confusions. The last thing the group needed was more of a challenge.

Calev handed Ona the new torch. He'd wrapped a ripped piece of his fine tunic around the end and smeared it with some plant growing at the base of the boulder where Kinneret and Miach sat. It burned hot and bright white.

A torch in her hand and her knife on her belt, Ona started across the makeshift bridge. The limbs shifted with her weight and the moon cast deceitful shadows across the uneven surface. Her wounds burned. The one from the battlefield throbbed in time with her heartbeat. It was a serious distraction and threw off her normally above-average balance. Three steps. Four.

One limb snapped.

Ona jerked. She fell straight down, through the branches until one leg was trapped between two of the tree limbs. She let out a very nasty curse.

"I was hoping that wouldn't happen. Too many bowls of Kurakian chicken with Seren..." she whispered to herself in Silvanian, trying to laugh off her fear.

Shaking and pleased she had managed to keep a hold on the torch, she tried to breathe deeply to calm herself. If fear took her here, it was over. A drop from this height was death. The ground was nothing but a great hole of darkness. There would be no getting out of that alive. Her knuckles whitened around the torch.

"You can do this, Onaratta." Dante's voice rumbled in their

native tongue. "You are a chanter. A true mercenary of Silvania. This little chore is nothing to someone like you."

Her heart swelled at the compliment even though she knew she didn't deserve it. "You never even saw me fight." She gripped the unbroken limbs and began lifting her body to draw her leg from its trap.

"Didn't I?"

She stared at Dante. "You said you found me half dead at the end of the battle." She felt oddly exposed, imagining this kind man watching her chant and strike and take the enemy down— his own fellow warriors down.

"That was the truth. But I also saw you. Right when you came onto the field."

Ona's foot found a solid surface behind her other foot. She stood slowly, face burning with the effort and concentration. The earth scent from below wafted into her nose and she wondered for a moment whether or not one could smell distance.

"Ona." Dante's voice was sharp. "Hurry up now, and I'll tell you exactly what I saw on that field of blood."

Swallowing, she took a tentative step. Another. "Did you hear the chants I used?"

"I did. I will never forget the image of you that day."

"Oh. I'm sure. Small mercenary falling on a sword. Very inspiring."

"That is not what I saw."

"Then tell me what you saw. A monster enraged beyond reason? A beast who defied her friends and let revenge take her straight into death's arms?"

Five more steps.

"No."

"Tell me."

"Keep walking."

Ona glanced down.

"Please," Dante said.

She leapt into his hands and they tumbled to the ground. The torch went flying.

Rolling, he held her gently on top of him. "I saw a goddess of protection, there to keep that city of innocents safe from Invaders and their desperate swords." His lips curved into a vicious smile. "You were stunning. You were so quick. You were the Empire's strongest weapon."

It wasn't true, but Ona couldn't seem to argue. She was all too aware of his strong body under hers and the feel of his hands on her hips.

Calev, Kinneret, and Miach waved their encouragement from the other side, and Ona spun away from Dante to find her feet as well as the torch.

"If we didn't have living trees and their heinous god after us, I'd have stayed there on that ground with you for a while." Ona grinned, feeling for once like herself.

Dante barked a laugh. "If I still have a proper body when this is all over, I'd be happy to give you a second chance."

And there it was. Ona was flirting properly again. A smile pulled her mouth wide, and she took out her dagger to spin it like she used to do when walking with Lucca in the forest.

The weight of the weapon was as familiar as her own fingers, but the handling of it didn't give her the same feeling it used to. Now, it was a blade that she might have to use against those who might hurt her or her friends. There was joy in the skill of wielding it—the spin and the clean striking movement —but she had no desire to drive it into anyone, even an enemy.

She gripped the weapon tightly, then stopped and stared at the thing.

Was this how Lucca had always felt about fighting? Was this the feeling he had and why he explained the reasons for each skirmish or battle to himself as they rode into a fight? No wonder he kept his books with him. Knowledge was what drove his soul. Not violence or rage or fierce pain.

What drove her soul?

The mural she'd started in the Napo Chapel flashed through her memory. The charcoal lines of wings, sunlight, and grape vines swirled in her mind's eye. She had brought the scene from Silvanian history to life with her own hands. The proud tilt of the queen's chin. A rock dove lifting into the sky. She'd brought that to life.

Her soul pulsed inside her chest, bringing her strength and driving the pain in her wounds away.

The knife glinted in the moonlight.

"I wish it was a paintbrush."

Her admission shocked her as much as it obviously did Dante. His look of confusion was comical to say the least.

"Don't wear that face too long," she said. "It might stick and then you'd have a hard time talking me into that *second chance.*" A laugh floated from her lips.

The rocky ground led them to a flat area. An opening yawned in the hill and musty air blew from inside.

"I'm sorry, but did I hear you say you wish your knife was a paintbrush? Am I going mad?"

The dark thickened inside the cave's entrance. Ona held out the torch and felt a moment of regret as Dante pulled a flint and stone from his pouch to re-light it. She would still be by Lucca's side if she hadn't turned to the wrong leader before the battle.

What would he say about her wish to turn her knife into a paintbrush?

"I used to be an artist," she said. "Before the Invaders killed my aunt. Before I ran to the mercenaries and gave my life to revenge." The torch's light illuminated spider webs on the ceiling and strange charred markings that might've been art from Miach's time. "I painted murals."

"That's impressive."

"Are you being sarcastic?"

"I'm not. Art is the key to civilization, if you ask me."

Ona tried not to chuckle, but she couldn't hide it. Dante frowned, facing her.

"I'm sorry," she said, still laughing. "But you're all *I'm the big warrior man and I'm a tracker and look at all my muscles* and now you're going on about art and civilization."

The light flickered over Dante's proud nose and the frown in the light-colored beard he'd grown since their flight from the other Invaders. Complicated shades of chestnut, copper, and wheat shone brightly in his tied-back hair. "Did you think Lucca was the only one with a brain in my family?"

"No. No. I'm so sorry." The old Ona would've hit him in the stomach and told him to get over it. New Ona actually realized she'd hurt his feelings and felt bad about it. "Really. You have proven your smarts over and over again. I'm a horse's arse. Sorry."

"You're fine. Just remember the cover doesn't always tell the story."

A shock of recognition flew through Ona. "Did you just quote Lucca?"

"Ah. No. That was originally from our mother. She gave Lucca his love of books."

The cave path turned left. Ona lifted the torch to keep them from losing their footing along the edge of the crevasse where the waterfall once fell. Now the area was dry as bone though the air had a musky dampness to it. Far off, drips of water echoed every several minutes.

"Lucca told me your mother wasn't overly…cozy."

Dante sniffed. "No. She wasn't horrible like our father, but she didn't seem to care too much about children. She was always running off to parties with nobles and other wealthy families. Most women seem to have children fairly young, but our mother had us when she was well past average childbearing years. I'm quite sure she is gone by now."

"I'm sorry."

"Don't be. I mourned her long ago and we were never close."

"Still."

Dante nodded, then paused. "Eh. Look up there."

Ona raised the torch, and a rough circle appeared in the cave's wall. A large point had grown down from the top of the opening, maybe from the small drips of water depositing minerals.

"Maybe little Miach could slip under that point, but I can't. Not without losing some skin." She banged the bottom of the torch against the stony growth

Dante took the torch. "Maybe let's not get lost in a dark cave, hm?"

She smiled. "But I can't get through there without breaking that point out of the way."

Dante handed the torch back to her, his fingers rubbing hers. She had the fleeting desire to curl her hand over his and—

He removed the sword from his belt and flipped it to show

the hilt. "If this thing can take down those tree monsters, I doubt it'll have too much trouble with a stalactite."

"A what?"

"Stalactite." He banged the hilt against the stone. It did nothing.

"Well, it doesn't seem to want to leave its happy home."

Dante sighed. "You're going to cut yourself pretty good getting in there." His years with Invaders had affected his accent in interesting ways. Ona had to remind herself that he wasn't one of them. He was a good man and he'd saved her more than once since they'd met.

"I don't have much of a choice. Your big self definitely won't fit."

"Did anyone ever tell you that your ability to compliment is severely lacking?"

"Let me rephrase. That tiny space can't possibly handle the magnificence of your extremely well-muscled and manly body."

"She can be taught, folks."

Ona punched him lightly in the stomach. "That felt nice." She popped her knuckles. "Maybe I'm not entirely finished with violence. It's so succinct. The light sock to the gut says it all."

He grinned. "And yet you're still talking."

"Heft me up there, please."

"You're sure?" His light eyes reflected the torch's flickering yellow. "Because this is going to hurt. We could maybe—"

Ona looked away from his beautiful eyes, from the fire reflecting in their depths. "There's no other way. We don't have time to be clever."

"As you wish." Dante got on all fours and jerked his head at his back.

Ona used the torch to study the opening once more before

propping it against some rocks. Dante's back muscles tightened under her boots. She slipped a bit, but managed to get her head through the circle of rock, then her arms and most of her torso. The stalactite bit into the back of her arm as she scraped through. Tumbling to the ground, darkness fell over her like she'd dropped into a giant ink pot.

"Little light, please?" She dusted grit from her clothing and stood to see Dante's face, peering at her alongside the torch.

"All right? How's the arm?"

Blood ran hot down to her elbow. "Not a problem."

Dante extended the torch through the opening and Ona took it. The orange light flickered along the uneven ceiling where a few tiny, dark green bats hung. Most of their friends were probably out hunting. That was just fine. A funny memory hit her. Lucca actually liked the flying rats. He'd spent one summer spouting facts about them after reading some monk's journal he bought at a market in the south.

The musky air didn't allow for a nice, deep breath like Ona's body needed. She tried to stay calm as the torch dimmed. Her feet stood in a few inches of dust.

"I don't see a shield."

"Maybe he tucked it into a corner?" Dante's voice echoed off the walls.

"You all right out there in the dark?"

"Yes, but I do think the bats are on their way back home."

Before she could say a thing, a flurry of wings exploded through the opening and crowded the ceiling. The creatures squeaked and swooped low. Ona's heart knocked against her teeth, and she ducked.

"They're luminescent!" Dante called out.

Ona reluctantly raised her head. Indeed, dotted lines of

glowing green ran down the bats' sides. "Focus. Where should I look? And how long is this torch going to last?" She squat-marched to the left, to a corner. "Any good guesses on that?"

"Calev smeared it with a root that should burn a bit longer than oil would. That was a good find. I may need to visit Old Farm with this new life I've been given. They know their plants."

Ona waved a curious bat away from her head. "Great. Sounds good."

Then her boot hit something.

She shoved her fingers into the thick cave dust and found a cool lip of worked metal.

"Dante."

"Yes?"

"You'll want to prepare a celebratory dance. I think I just found the key to defeating Runnos."

There was a roar. A crack.

The cave shook.

Something hit Ona and the world went black.

17

KINNERET

The ground shifted under Kinneret's feet.

Miach shrieked and clung to Ethus. "I told you he would know. He is going to kill us!"

But this couldn't be Runnos, could it? They were past the boundary. This might've been the earth shaking like it did sometimes in this area. Like the activity that altered the waterfall and took the town Ona had mentioned.

The earth jerked again. The cave across from the branching chasm expelled a cloud of dust in the moonlight.

"Calev!" Kinneret was already running toward the chasm and the bridge.

Miach pulled at her hand, but his strength was nothing to hers and no matter how much she did indeed worry about what Runnos would do to them during this whole thing, she couldn't let something happen to Dante and Ona—they'd risked their lives to save Oron, a man they didn't even know.

Calev joined her at the bridge, and they panted as the earth calmed and the dust cleared. A cloud whisked past the moon, then scant silver light drifted over the mouth of the cave.

The opening was gone.

The cave was nothing but a pile of rock.

Miach was sniffling quietly. His goat sat on his feet. "I hate this meadow," he whispered.

Kinneret's heart tilted and pressed against her side. "I know. Me too. Calev, I can't let them die in there."

"Certainly not." He wiped his hair away from his face, then seemed to realize he'd lost his headtie at some point. "I'll go over. Maybe there is a path out that we can't see. I can call out to them and maybe help them move in the right direction."

But Kinneret knew who was the strongest here. Even with the dizziness, it was her. With this curse running through her veins, she held power in her arms, legs, and hands that she'd never even imagined. Knowing full well Calev would argue, she didn't ask his advice before vaulting over the crevasse in one graceful leap.

The only sounds were Calev's gasp of surprise and water rushing somewhere far, far, far below her morphing body.

She landed with a thud and hurried to the cave. The rockfall had no obvious room for escape. "Dante! Ona!"

Calev said her name once, but then both he and Miach kept quiet on the other side of the abyss so she could hear, but no voices answered except the distant whisper of the forest and the green men's buzzing like gnats she couldn't shake out of her ears.

The rockfall consisted of mostly large, slanted cuts of rock that had sheered from the outcropping above the cave. After a quick glance back at Calev, she curled her branching fingers around one of the rocks. It was nearly the size of her own torso,

147

but it was light as a bundle of wheat in her new arms. She turned and threw it into the chasm.

She didn't want to see what Calev's face showed right now as she removed another rock. He had to be shocked at the change in her. This strength—more than the pine needles growing along her temples and flaring from her eyelashes, or the spindly look of her fingers—said very clearly that she was no longer human.

Swallowing panic, she worked up a sweat heaving rocks from the former opening and calling out for Dante and Ona like her life depended on it. Because it did. Her human life would be gone soon if the shield and sword didn't beat Runnos down. Oron would die. Avi would be without a sister. Calev, Miach, Ona, Dante, and probably even poor little Ethus, would all die an ugly death at the hands of the green men. Pulled apart. Absorbed into the trees for their lifeblood.

She couldn't think about that now. She would succeed in this. Everyone needed her and she flat-out refused to fail. She was Kaptan Kinneret Raza, and she would not go down this way.

Flinging the last of the rock away, she rushed into the cave's dusty mouth. "Dante! Onaratta!"

"Here!" Dante's voice was close. He coughed in the darkness.

A torch. Why hadn't she brought a new torch? Of course theirs was out. She kept her back against the wall and walked over fallen rocks, heading deeper into the hill.

"Wave one of those long arms of yours toward the ceiling," Dante said.

"What? Why?" What possible purpose could there be to that? It might even damage the cave further. Maybe he'd been hit on the head.

"The bats. They're in here. I can hear them. Listen. They're luminescent. If we disturb them, I think they'll light up."

Kinneret frowned, but did as he said and reached high to run fingers above her head. The ceiling exploded into a flurry of wings and a green glow. It didn't amount to much light, but a circle of stone showed above the place where Dante stood.

Blood ran down the warrior's cheek and under his chin. "She is in there." He pointed a thumb toward the circle in the cave wall.

Kinneret stepped over another pile of rubble and leaned in through the circle. A point of rock scraped her skull lightly. No moonlight or light from the bats reached the space beyond the opening. "Ona?"

Ona coughed, and Kinneret jumped, knocking her chin on the rock. "I'm here," Ona said. She sounded terrible.

"Did you find the shield?"

"Yes. I…here…hold on." There was a scraping sound and the shield appeared. Ona wedged it through the space sideways.

"Here, let me," Dante said, taking hold of the shield.

Even in the dark, Kinneret could tell the shield was dented and very dusty. Dante worked the circle of metal through the space.

"You ready to crawl out of there, Ona?" Dante's voice was strong and direct, like he was doing his best to make Ona feel like it was a surety that she would actually be able to get back out of that other room. "How can we help?"

"My entire body hurts like I've been run over by a very large creature with too many legs. But I think I can manage."

The dark hid her progress, but with the grunting and scraping and occasional cursing, Kinneret was fairly sure she was getting through.

"Take a swipe at those creepy bats again, will you?" Ona asked. "I need to see where to drop what with all these new rocks."

Kinneret waved her hands high, ignoring the fact that her arms were distinctly longer than they were supposed to be.

The tiny flying mammals bloomed into light, and Dante hurried past Kinneret to help Ona to their side of the cave. Using mostly feel and the small splash of moonlight the cave's new look allowed, the group worked their way outside.

Calev's smile was bright in the low light. But Kinneret knew most of his good mood was forced. He had to have been struck by how she leapt across the crevasse earlier. "I am *very* glad to see all of you."

"How about this?" Ona held the shield up proudly, and it flashed moonlight across Miach's face and Ethus's hooves.

Calev clapped. "We are well armed now, friends. Now, how are you going to get back across?"

Kinneret swallowed the disgust she felt about her changing form, grabbed Ona and Dante in one arm each, then vaulted over the chasm as easily as if it was a mud puddle in the Jakobden marketplace.

18

ONA

The one-thousand-year-old shield may've been the dustiest item Ona had ever held, but under its layer of dirt, it was glorious, just like the sword. There were several dents beside one of the bronze circles set into the steel but the runes etched in each circle were clear-cut and practically hummed with power. She ran her hand over one of the stones set into the bronze circles. Most of them felt relatively the same, but even in the near dark she could tell they were different colors.

"How will it work exactly?" Dante asked Miach as they crossed the meadow.

"We shouldn't have it," Miach said. "He will hate this."

"But you do know how it works." Ona smiled encouragingly.

"Father set the stones for a clear mind, focus, blocking negativity, and grounding. Malachite, smoky quartz, clear quartz, hematite, and amazonite."

"So the stones are what blocks Runnos's influence on the bearer?"

"Yes, but it won't work. It will only protect those under it. And not all of us can fit. Besides, the green men can still grab you. The shield doesn't stop that."

"Are you a sorcerer like your father was?" Calev's gaze was on Kinneret even as he spoke to the boy. His eyes were always turned in her direction. "I've never met a sorcerer."

"Yes, you have," Kinneret said gently. "At the dock in Verita. You met that Northern Isle seithr. They are sorcerers, right?"

"I didn't realize they were the same thing. I suppose you could be deemed a sorcerer too, my fire."

Miach wrinkled his nose. "Aren't there sorcerers in every town?"

"Not anymore," Dante said. "My mother once told me the northern air somehow gives such powers. But it must not blow around like it used to, because there are only people who do amazing things with runes and stones in the Northern Isles now, and they can only work their magic near their homeland. Mostly. At least, that's what my mother told me when I was little."

"My grandfather was the most powerful sorcerer ever." Miach beamed, but then his smile faded. "But he died long before I was even born."

"What killed a man that strong?" Kinneret asked.

Miach scratched his head. "I don't remember. My father told me, but I...can't remember the story."

"It must've been a great story." Calev gave Miach a sad smile.

"It was. And father used his caster to show it to me."

Ona handed the shield to Dante. Her injuries were throbbing. "What is a caster?"

"It's a length of woven thread," Miach said. "Done in threes and sevens."

Kinneret stopped. "Like a wraith lantern's wick."

"Yes. Exactly." Miach grinned up at Kinneret.

"The caster showed Father's story in the colors of the weaving. It was all in blue and white so I didn't get to see it like true life, but it was amazing anyway. At least, I think it was…"

"What's wrong?" Ona pulled his finger from his mouth. He'd started chewing a nail.

"There is a blank spot in my own memory. I can't remember the casting Father did of Grandfather's death. I think he showed it to me. Maybe I…I don't know."

"It's all right," Calev said gently. "Just rest. Maybe you'll remember tomorrow. We should stop to sleep."

"I agree that we should stop," Ona said. "I can barely put one foot in front of the other."

GUIDED by Calev and using his flint and dagger, they built a small fire solely out of fallen, fully dead branches and old logs. Dante and Calev stood watch while Kinneret, Miach, Ethus, and Ona found spots around the fire to shut their eyes for a bit.

Ona couldn't seem to sleep.

Mostly because of the monsters just waiting to attack from the green shadows, but also because the woman next to her was quickly growing into one of those monsters. Kinneret dozed, her forehead wrinkled in the firelight. Tipped in long pine needles, her eyelashes brushed over her cheeks. She'd tucked her knees up and her feet moved slowly as she slept. But they weren't feet. They'd become roots. Each toe had elongated into a searching twist of woody root and Ona wouldn't have been surprised if they plunged into the earth right now to soak up nutrients from the ground.

How long would it be safe to be around Kinneret?

The woman's hands were frightening too. Ona shut her eyes to stop staring. Those hands had saved slaves, rescued a sister, and worked salt and prayers like no one in history. It was so sad that this might be her end. With a heaviness hanging on her heart, Ona's body finally overruled her mind and she fell into a deep, dreamless sleep.

A shout woke her. It was nearly dawn.

Ona jumped to her feet, body responding properly for once. A green man with a beard of oak leaves snarled and his branching arm reached for Dante's leg. As Dante fell, he threw his shield to Ona. Her hands moved to catch it. She slipped her arm through the leather strap and had one fleeting thought about the magic that held leather in one piece for one thousand years.

Dante struck at the bearded tree spirit with the runed sword. The creature dropped back.

In the pre-dawn light, Calev threw dirt into a tall, thin green man's eyes, then rushed to the fire. He grabbed up a burning stick.

"Good thinking!" Ona went for her own piece of flaming wood.

Kinneret stood and held her hands over her ears, tears streaming down her cheeks. "The entire continent. All the forests and all the towns. You can't. No!"

There was no time to figure out what Kinneret was talking about.

Ona gritted her teeth against the pain in her wounds and teamed up with Calev to light the tall green man's shoulder and torso on fire. The thing shrieked and spun, nearly toppling onto Miach and Ethus, who'd tucked themselves behind Dante. Dante was up and fighting again, the sword moving quickly but not quickly enough.

Ona pulled her flint from her belt.

Then the voices of the wood shouted into everyone's heads. Ona heard it too.

Give in to us. We are your life. You are our life. Rest. Rest. Rest.

Miach pointed at the shield with a tiny finger. "Ona!"

She lifted the shield above her head. The voices disappeared. All she heard was the hiss of roots sliding over the ground, the moaning of the green man who they'd burned, and the cackle of the bearded tree spirit.

Kinneret was tossing her head violently and crying like she'd lost everything already.

Dante wasn't using that sword of his the way she could. The way she used to.

It was time to see if she still had her skills buried deep inside of her. "Calev! Flint please!" He tossed her the stone. "Dante! Sword!" She reached out a hand.

He blinked, then tossed the weapon hilt first.

Catching it neatly, she began a chant.

"Your enemy is my enemy,

Let him feel my wrath."

Her lips trembled as she struck the flint on her sword.

"I strike like the snake."

A flame leapt from her hands, and she clutched the flint in her shield hand as she spun and dragged the runed sword across the tall green man's scorched middle. He screamed and crumpled to the ground.

"I bite like the wolf."

155

She ran at the green man coming at Dante, her knees like jelly. The creature raised a leafed hand as she jabbed the sword under his arm, deep into his trunk-like torso. The thing roared. She dropped the weapon and the shield both.

The green man bled sharp-scented sap as he dragged himself toward her. Her hands shook so hard that she couldn't even try to pick up the blade. She was going to die here, taken down like she'd never fought a day in her life.

"I'm no warrior," she said, somehow needing to voice the truth. To accept it.

A large hand darted forward, grabbed the runed sword, then plunged it into the green man's back. Dante stood over the thing as it curled and twitched, dying beside the smoldering fire.

Sweating and flushed, Calev grabbed the shield and held it out to Kinneret. She was still wailing and covering her ears. "Try this, my fire. Try this." Tears welled in his eyes.

She twisted to look at him. Now, she stood taller than he did. Her strange fingers reached out for the shield, desperation plain on her face.

"Runnos showed me it all," she whispered. "He isn't only enforcing his rule here, in this wood. He is somehow connected to all the other forests. Everywhere." Her face paled. "All the green men are waking. Runnos will destroy every city in Silvania, Jakobden, Old Farm—the entire Empire."

Bile touched the back of Ona's throat.

The entire continent.

That's what Kinneret had been screaming during the fight. Runnos planned to overtake humankind completely. Ona's mind flew to Lucca and Seren.

Would Seren see this possibility in the Fire? What would she do in Ona's situation?

Calev was very obviously shaken. He glanced at the surrounding trees, then held the shield out to Kinneret again.

She took it.

The moment her flesh touched the shield, her mouth fell open into a silent scream. Dropping the shield, she went to her knees and Calev wrapped his arms around her.

Dante swallowed hard, also moving his gaze away from Calev and Kinneret, and offered his hand to Ona. She took it, but didn't stand. Instead, she pulled him down next to her to sit. Miach and Ethus snuggled up behind her and began playing with sticks in the fire.

"Could Runnos truly take over everything?" Dante asked quietly.

"Who knows? Maybe." Nausea poured through her. "We have no way to warn anyone." The wind tugged her hair, and she let it, too weary in body and soul to care about much of anything. "I...I thought I could chant again. And save you all. I couldn't even hold a weapon."

"You killed that one." Dante nodded toward the scorched and dead tall green man. "And nearly offed this one too. You just needed a little back up. Get it? I stabbed him in the back so...?"

Ona smiled warily, too overwhelmed to let him cheer her up with terrible jokes.

"Eh, Onaratta. Come here." Dante opened his arms.

Eyes burning, she went into them gratefully. Dante waved for Miach join their small circle. They huddled together for a few quiet minutes.

Ona tried to imagine a way out of this, but she just couldn't.

Not with Oron alive, Miach freed, and Kinneret as a human again. Dante met her gaze. She traced the sweep of his eyebrows and the turn of his cheek. She touched his bottom lip, wishing she could mix a color to match the exact shade of his handsome mouth, wishing she was far away, paintbrush or chalk in hand.

This situation was hopeless.

Runnos wanted a war, and Ona had realized her passion didn't lay in being a warrior. She was, and always had been, an artist.

19

KINNERET

K inneret's mind finally eased and Runnos left her
alone again. The quiet was wonderful. She pulled it
in desperately, almost like she breathed air after a
deep, deep dive. Without the terror and seductive tug of
Runnos in her head, she could think through what she'd just
experienced. There was almost too much to untangle. She
clenched her hands together.

Runnos was going for all of it. The human world would fall
under his roots.

Unless they stopped him. Here. Now.

If she were to organize a group to take down an age-old
god, this wouldn't be it. Yes, they had Dante and Ona, but the
rest of them were simply a boy, a farmer, a sailor, and a goat.
But Ona...

During the fight, Ona had moved faster than anyone should
ever be able to move. When she spoke those Silvanian words—
her chant, she'd called them—she'd practically flown over the

ground to attack the green men. She'd only been a blur most of the time.

"Ona. You are amazing."

Ona closed her eyes.

Kinneret let her be. The mercenary was obviously not pleased with her performance during the fight, but Kinneret remained completely impressed. If that was disappointing, she couldn't even imagine how the woman fought at peak level.

Miach scooted toward his father's shield and began touching each stone in turn. "Malachite." The swirling green of the rock reminded Kinneret of the water around Old Farm's dock. "Clear quartz and smoky quartz." Miach's thumb bounced along the stones. "They help with keeping your thoughts to yourself and keeping his thoughts away." He breathed warm air onto a silvery stone. "Hematite. My favorite. Which one do you like, Kinneret?"

"That last one." She pointed. "The one that looks like the Pass when the sun filters through it."

The memory of the day she, Oron, and Calev dove into the Pass to look for the wine jug and the map to Ayarazi washed through her. She could almost feel the cool water against her sand-worn skin. The sound of Calev's feet kicking through the waves. Oron's shout under the water because they didn't leave when he thought best.

She smiled and swallowed against the pain.

Oron was still trapped.

Did he know they were trying to save him? Doubtful. If Runnos wasn't sure what they were up to, Oron wouldn't catch wind of it. But what if Runnos simply didn't think they could pull it off? They had the sword and the shield. How long until Runnos brought down his entire army of green men?

Miach clicked an opaque, blue-green stone with a knuckle. "That's...ummm. It's a hard word. Sounds something like Zonite."

"Kin," Calev whispered into her ear, tickling her. She longed for simpler times when that was all she needed in the world. "Ask to look into his memory again. We need information."

He was right. "Miach? Would you mind if I peeked at your life again? At your memories? I promise to stop if you ask or if it makes you feel bad."

He took a heavy breath, then plopped into Kinneret's lap. "All right." He faced Ona. "But Ona, please watch Ethus until we're done."

"Will do." Circles hung below Ona's eyes, Dante's too.

They were all exhausted. Ona stared at the fallen green men. Kinneret refused to look at them.

"I'll gather some more food." Dante stood and began eyeing the surrounding area. "Calev, you want to join me?"

"I'm going to help Kinneret and Miach. Just in case."

Dante nodded and began picking his way into the brush, sword in hand.

Kinneret smiled at Miach, then placed her hands on his bare forearms. She closed her eyes and Miach's family appeared. They stood beside a large hut made of stone, moss, and sticks.

A fire snapped beside his father, who laughed at something Miach's uncle had said. Then his father held up his hands.

"Come close, kin. This is the only casting you'll see me do for a long while. I grow tired of the drain of magic. The air...it changes."

Miach-Kinneret toddled forward on chubby legs. He held onto his mother's brightly-dyed skirt. "What will you show? The ships? Show the ships."

Miach's father touched his nose. "No ships today. I will show you something far more important. This is the casting of the day my own father gave his life to contain Runnos."

Whispers ran through the small crowd of dark-headed cousins and siblings.

Miach's mother chewed her lip and the boy pulled on her skirt. The fabric was coarse and familiar.

"Don't you like this story, Mother?"

"I don't. I miss that man. Your grandfather."

Miach hugged her leg, bunching the fabric, as his father turned a large loom to face the group. The thick woolen threads woven from end to end, side to side, held two colors—a soft blue and an ivory shade. The chieftain spread his fingers wide and touched the yarn. The loom shivered. The wool almost seemed to spark in the firelight. Father stepped to the side a little, then traced shapes with his thumbs against the weave.

Runes.

Then Kinneret was struck with an invisible force. The memory flew away from her mind. Calev and Miach stared, saying something, but she couldn't hear them over Runnos's words in her head. The words echoed, purred, sucked at the marrow of her bones.

No. Listen to me. To me. Come to me.

There was a flash of movement, then Runnos's voice disappeared, and Calev's voice became clear.

"Was Runnos interrupting the memory?" Calev took her hand and stroked it gently like it was still her same old hand and not one twisted by a god.

"Ona fixed it." Miach grinned and pointed up.

Ona held the shield above Kinneret and Miach like a roof.

She smiled over the edge. "Try to see the memory again, Kinneret. I'll hold this here."

Kinneret drew up her courage and accepted little Miach from Calev. The boy smiled sadly and pressed a hand to her throat. His skin was warm and soft.

The memory flooded into her senses.

The scent of a fire. The jostle of people standing beside Miach on that day. The excitement running through Miach's blood as he watched his father cast.

The chieftain stepped out of the way of the loom and spoke in low, powerful tones.

"I cast the tale of my father. Great sorcerer. Strong father. Sacrifice for our safety."

The weaving began to move.

First, it was just a ripple that could be dismissed as wind moving the wool, but then the small movements became the shapes of a man and a deep valley filled with pines and bluebells. At the widest pine—a massive tree unlike any Kinneret had ever seen—the man lifted a staff and spoke, his voice unheard.

Miach's father spoke for the casting, explaining the images. "'I challenge you, Runnos, god of the wood, to do your best to kill me with your own breath.'"

The weaving showed five green men rush at the sorcerer.

"'Do not send your henchmen to do the job, Runnos!' my grandfather said, 'Use your own breath. Can you not do it, powerful god of the wood?'" Miach's father smirked and watched the woolen green men flinch from the sorcerer.

A huge wave of movement rolled through the weave. Miach's father took on the voice of Runnos. "'You are nothing to me.'"

The limbs of the huge pine in the center of the valley stretched. What looked like a cloud billowed from the shadows hanging from the tree.

The sorcerer held up a staff. He quickly dragged the tip of it through the air to form a complicated series of dips, loops, and slashes as the cloud tumbled toward him.

Miach held his breath, fingers tightly gripping his mother's skirt.

The cloud hit the runes his grandfather had drawn in the air.

The plumes of power froze, then shattered into shining pieces.

The brilliant white specks of the former cloud overtook the sorcerer, and he crumbled at the base of the pine. Filling the entire valley, the sparkling cloud morphed into a strange liquid that increased and increased until the entire weaving was the pale white of the moon.

Miach's father faced his family. "And that is how my father died. He battled the great Runnos, shook the god well, but in the end, lost that fight."

The memory slid out of Kinneret's head. She blinked, then saw Miach's sweet face, older than he was in the memory, and Calev just behind him, eyes fierce with worry.

A sharp knowledge swept over Kinneret. "I know where the sacred grove lies."

Miach's mouth dropped open. He tried to speak, probably to confirm what Kinneret had put together from the memory and the information they'd already gathered.

"Where is it?" Dante walked up, holding two fistfuls of green plants.

Kinneret closed her eyes and wished Runnos's heart—his

sacred grove—was somewhere other than the place that would forever haunt her nightmares, if she lived long enough to have nightmares.

In that silver pool, she had started her transition into a monster. The moment her toe hit that cursed water, she'd lost her entire life and everyone in it.

"The sacred grove…" She coughed, then cleared her throat. "It's under the silver pool."

Calev stood. "The place that cursed you?"

Kinneret nodded.

Miach nervously twirled the longer hairs on Ethus's foreleg with a finger.

Kinneret set a gentle hand on his back. "Miach. Don't feel bad about not knowing. It's not your job to know everything. You already told us so much. You are the reason we found the shield. You are the reason Runnos is going to lose this fight with us."

The side of Miach's mouth lifted and he kissed Ethus right between the goat's tiny horns. He whispered something to his little friend. They both jumped up, Miach grabbed the shield from Ona, then he and the goat disappeared into the forest.

Dante ran after them.

Ona's eyes were wide. "I just let him have it. I didn't know he was going to run."

Calev started after Dante, calling out Miach's name.

"Why would he leave like that?" Kinneret trailed Calev. "Or if he was going to betray us, why not take the sword too?"

Ona followed Kinneret through a thicket of thorny undergrowth. "He's a boy. He would barely be able to lift that sword. It's much heavier than the shield."

Low tree branches swayed in Dante and Calev's wake,

Kinneret ducked low to avoid a larger pine's branch, and Ona climbed over a fallen log.

"Miach!" Kinneret's voice was lower and scratchier than it should've been.

Beyond a stretch of beech trees, Dante knelt. He touched the ground, then turned. "They're headed east."

"But why?" Ona squeezed her hands into fists. She'd messed with her hair at some point and the two knots she wore were neater and more tightly wound. Mud still showed on her face and her eyes were bloodshot. "He's going to get himself killed," Ona said.

"Not killed. Punished maybe. Runnos can't undo making him immortal, can he?" Calev grabbed Kinneret's hand as they hurried under a tangle of mossy, oak limbs.

Dante and Ona zipped through the wood ahead of them, crouched and ready to spring at whatever might come at them.

"Who knows?" Kinneret said in answer to Calev's question about Runnos snatching immortality away. "He gave it. Why couldn't he take it away?"

"We should've worked harder to convince him we're going to win against Runnos and free him."

"That would've been difficult considering I'm seriously doubting it at this point. How can any of us get through that silver pool to the grove hiding underneath? The water," she stopped to swallow her fear, "takes over your mind and nearly paralyzes you."

Calev rubbed at the beard trying to grow over his sharp jawline. "But if the person who tries to breach the watery boundary holds the shield, maybe they'd be protected."

"Like the shield protected me as I watched Miach's memory."

"Exactly."

"It's not a bad idea, Master of the Harvest." Kinneret grinned teasingly. When Calev explained things or gave orders, his voice deepened and sounded more like his father's. Kinneret teased him about it, but really, she liked the sound of it. The authority inside the tone was like a special power. And anything that gave Calev power was fine by her.

Calev rolled his eyes. "I was not using that voice."

"You were."

"No."

"Definitely." She ran a finger along his arm, pretending not to notice how her skin no longer looked like her skin at all. It'd do no good to fall apart right now. It was better to joke and plan and grit teeth than to moan and wail about what she'd lost. Once she was fully a green man, then she could mourn.

Calev huffed and shook his head. "Fine. Back to the point. One of us will enter the silver pool and—"

Ona ran back toward them. "Calev, may I ask you something? Privately?" She made an apologetic look in Kinneret's general direction.

Kinneret froze, anger ready to fly but reason holding it back. "Why?"

Ona breathed out slow as Dante continued on, his form just a small mark of light in the emerald trees. "You're turning into one of them. Runnos speaks to you through thoughts. Who is to say he can't take everything Calev is telling you about possible strategy right out of your head?"

It was like falling to the ship's decking and knocking her chin on the planks.

She stepped toward Ona, chest heaving. "So you've given up

on me, have you? Think I'm already one of them? Well, I'm not, and I know how to protect my own thoughts."

Ona backed away, chin high to look up at Kinneret. "You have to admit Runnos has full access to your mind some of the time."

Calev worked his way between them. "Ona, give us a moment?"

Ona sighed and started the way Dante had gone. Kinneret was very, very glad to see the back of her. The mercenary scared her a little. The way she'd moved during her attempt at chanting when she fought the green man attacking Dante...

"Kinneret, I can see you're weighing the idea of knocking Ona's head from her shoulders."

"She is a really great fighter."

"And that's the only thing holding you back."

"Pretty much."

"Not the fact that she risked her life to save us."

Kinneret glared. "She also thinks I'm going to betray you, the love of my life, to Runnos."

"She doesn't think you'll do it on purpose."

A grinding sounded in Kinneret's jaw. "Kind of her."

"You did lose your control for a moment earlier."

"And I fought him and won it back."

"What if it takes longer for you to win it back next time and he picks around in your thoughts and beats us before we even have a chance to try a plan, any plan?"

He was right. Of course he was right. But Kinneret was not in the mood to say so. She stormed away, her hair longer now and trailing pine needles. Sprigs of the same green growth emerged above her elbows, on the back of her arms. Swallowing, she tried to tug them off. It hurt like they were another appendage. Like she was trying to pull her own arms off.

Heat swirled inside her middle and crawled up her throat. Anger crashed over her like a wave. She thrashed in the current of her fear and outrage and frustration, ripping at the needles in her hair and kicking her root-like legs and feet. Great mounds of earth flew from the piles of dead needles as she tore through the wood toward Ona.

"I won't let him take me! I refuse!"

One sound stopped her, reined in her rage.

"Kinneret." It was Oron.

They had returned to the grove where Oron stood trapped inside a broken pine. She and Calev ran to the tree. None of Oron was visible, but they could hear his wheezing gasp and the one word he managed to utter.

"Kinneret."

Her anger poured out of her eyes in the form of tears. "Oron. We're here. We're going to get you out. Stay strong. It's almost over."

She gripped Calev's wrist, then hurried to follow Dante and Ona. They could talk all they wanted without her. As long as they let her stay to fight as long as she was still in control of her body. The insult and hurt Ona's comment had caused was nothing compared to the panic that hearing Oron had raised inside her.

As they picked their way through the unnaturally darker part of the forest, Kinneret turned to Calev. She memorized the fierce glint in his eyes and the firm set of his jaw.

"Do whatever you think is best," she said quietly. "You and Ona and Dante. Keep me out of it if you think you should. I don't care. We just have to get Oron out of there."

ALISHA KLAPHEKE

Calev paused to touch her lips, her cheek, her eyelids. "You are an amazing woman."

Before she could respond, he tugged her gently, urging her to move quickly.

Soon they'd caught up to the two warriors.

They stood a good distance from the silver pool. The water lay utterly silent. Not a ripple despite the chilly, resin-scented breeze. Ona had one hand on Dante's shoulder.

In front of them, close to the pool and beyond arm's reach, Miach held the shield above his head. His little arms hardly seemed substantial enough to do the job. Ethus stood beside him, preternaturally still for a baby goat. The sun that fought its way through the canopy and the forest's heavy gloom glinted off the stones of the shield—green, clear, gray, silver, and blue.

Miach and Ethus walked into the pool of cursed water.

20

KINNERET

Hands grabbed Kinneret's hair and dragged her backward, her strange feet digging rows into the earth. She screamed and heard Dante shout something.

Green men were everywhere.

An oaken man lashed a leafy paw at Ona. Blackish green leaves scattered into the wind as he knocked her off her feet. She began to chant in Silvanian as she lunged at the thing. Despite her speed, it slipped to the side of her blade. Her chant faded, and she stood there like she was frozen.

"Just stab him and be done with it!" Kinneret shouted, her own scalp burning as the tree spirit pulled her to standing.

Another green man, with pinecones framing his face, ran at Calev.

Kinneret's heart beat sickeningly in her throat. She swung at the green man holding her, but couldn't reach his face. One finger caught in the branches sprouting from its shoulders and snapped out and back into place with a shot of pain.

The green man rammed his head into Calev's side. Calev flew several feet before crashing into another tree. He stayed down.

Kinneret swayed. "Calev?" Her voice, like her body, felt sick and wrong. Calev was fine. He had to be. Avi needed him. She needed him.

Three green men raised woody legs to splash into the silver pool after Miach and Ethus, who didn't seem to notice.

The water slid up Miach's arms and hit his chin.

The tree spirit holding Kinneret jerked her to the ground, then lifted one massive root to smash her into the ground.

Kinneret had a fleeting thought. Avi was safe in Jakobden. She'd go to the Gathering soon and meet with the boy who'd helped her during her visit to Akhayma. She'd be happy. At least there was that.

Because it was now certain that Kinneret was about to die.

Dante flipped a different green man over his back. The creature landed beside Kinneret, green-black eyes rolling in its jade-tinted face. Dante slipped between Kinneret and the massive root. Grimacing, he drove the runed sword upward. The steel pierced the monster's foot. It howled and listed left as Dante pulled Kinneret to standing. Calev was up and fighting again. His dagger moved like small bolts of lightning in the storm of branches coming at him from all angles.

Two green men had him surrounded.

Kinneret coursed over the ground, fire in her veins. She reached for the first green man tearing at Calev and wrapped her new fingers around its neck. Her strength had increased, but she still couldn't pull the thing away from him.

Dante was there slashing the other green man's legs out from under him.

Kinneret gritted her teeth and tugged at the green man and finally, finally pulled him a step away from Calev. Two lines of blood leaked from Calev's nose.

Ona kicked a smaller green man away from her. She stood at the lip of the silver pool, hands cupped at her mouth and her hair in her eyes. "Miach! Behind you!"

The green men in the pool had only to reach out and they'd nearly have Miach. The milky water rose over Miach's black hair. It lipped over the shield. Covered Miach's knuckles.

And then the boy and his friend and the shield were gone.

The old sorcerer's broken spell—the silver pool of blessings and curses—swallowed them whole.

Kinneret yanked her victim back a step more, then squeezed as tightly as she could, choking the thing. Did it need air? The green man's face darkened. His lips went black. Bile rose in her throat as the fight left him, and he tumbled from her grasp. She was growing stronger every minute.

Yesssss.

"No!" she shouted at Runnos's voice in her head and dove into the fight with Calev and Dante.

Calev threw his dagger and missed. Kinneret ran for the blade. Found it stuck in the ground. Ripped it free and tossed it, end over end, to Calev. He threw again and this time it hit the target. The knife drove straight into the tree creature's eye. It shrieked, the sound like a murder of crows in Kinneret's ears. Dante's runed sword whipped low, then high. He jumped and twisted at an angle, slicing the back of the green man's neck. The creature fell to its knees.

Now, my new one. My strong one. Now. Be with me. We will rule the forest as one.

Sudden as a storm at night, Kinneret's mind fell under the god's sway.

Wholly.

Completely.

No space left untended, untouched.

Runnos's words spilled down Kinneret's temples like warm oil. They slid over her neck and down her body. She shivered. It felt as though the god's request, his demand, soaked into her. His will was her will. There was no fighting it.

"Kinneret!" A familiar voice broke through Runnos's continued whispering.

She shook her head hard and tried to form Calev's name in her mind and on her lips.

A hand touched her, and she looked down to see him. Her love. She smiled, and Runnos's voice faded a little.

Dante raised the spelled sword and the light hit her eyes like arrows.

In her momentary blindness, Runnos's voice grew louder.

My strong one. My powerful soul. Fate brought you here.

The scent of pines billowed over her. Her body seemed to light up from the inside out. The sounds of rain on leaves and of trees creaking in the wind filled her ears to bursting. She was the forest. The forest was her. She felt every insect crawling just under the ground, along the roots. Each move of the night wind shifted her limbs. The oaks, beech, and pines sang for her, deep and dark and beautiful. The forest swamped her senses in a lush tangle of sound and feeling.

Let go. Fall in. Let go. Let go. Let go.

When she opened her eyes, she saw as Runnos and the other green men did. There were no fleshy, small creatures who thought and loved and had a purpose outside feeding the forest. There were only flames of life that made her mouth water for want of them.

Take them. Yes. They are all yours. Then, you go into the water.

The buzz and heat of power rushed over Kinneret's limbs and through her chest, to her heart. She opened her mouth. A roar that sounded like a great tree cracking open poured from her lips. Flinging her right hand out, each digit a bendable branch of dark green leaves and spiny twigs, she caught up one of the bright flames of life.

She was so thirsty.

Yes. Feed. Feed on these.

So very thirsty for life.

The moment the flame touched her toughened skin, she knew she'd never be satisfied. She could feast on these flickers of lights for an eternity and never, ever stop. Drawing the life toward her body, her trunk-like stomach tensing, she heard something just beyond the din of Runnos's smooth permission to continue feeding.

"Kinneret," a voice said from far, far away. "You are my fire. You are Avi's sister." Something in the voice reminded her of something… "You are a beautiful, strong salt worker who loves the sea. Remember. Please, my fire, remember."

Tears choked this strangely familiar voice. Kinneret's heart curled around the sounds from this flame of life. She paused. He was special. But she wasn't sure why. If she absorbed his life into her, she'd no longer hear his words.

Runnos spoke louder in her mind. *If he confuses you, break him and take him later. I need your power now, my strong one.*

The life in her hands struggled and cried out her name. Her name?

"Kinneret!"

Yes, it was.

She released the flame.

Runnos thundered inside her skull. *Then another of my green men will take him. He cannot be released.*

They would absorb the man's familiar light. His name...he was called...Calev! Calev. How did she know this flickering light's name? What was this? If one of the others took him, fed on him, Calev would be no more.

The thought bent her in half, and she coughed, hands going to her neck. Her skin was so tough, sharp, wrong. Nausea swam through her middle. She stumbled.

Then she was herself again.

Calev stood below her, hands raised. "We will beat this, my fire!"

She started to reach for him, smiling and weeping.

Runnos gripped her mind. *We will create a fresh earth.*

Images of bloodied swords and fighting men fell under a carpet of bright green grasses. In her mind, saplings burst through the ground. A parent hit a child, then the child tore the wings from a butterfly. A wave of leaves crashed over them, leaving only a peaceful land of birdsong and sunshine, of a forest as wide as the horizon itself. Again and again the images, like paintings, moved through Kinneret's head. Blood and gore and hate and evil—all washed in green.

This is what the land is. This is what our land could be.

Then she saw the continent, stretching from the far West to Verita's bustling port, from the ports north of here to the most southern reaches, beyond Jakobden and Old Farm. The entire landform rolled and shook like a great beast, crumbling cities with powerful tree limbs and thick vines of red-tinged ivy.

And though it was horrible, though it filled her with such terror, this new heat inside her knew it was beautiful.

Calev called her name. "Don't forget your sister, Avigail. Avi, who plays games and reads too much and loves you and needs you. Think of the night we were Intended. The love between us." He touched her, and she knew he was right.

She focused on Runnos's presence in her mind. "There is great beauty in us too. In humans."

She brought all her greatest memories to mind.

Small Avi, long ago, flinging herself at Kinneret for a hug after a long day at sea. Her little arms were so strong even then, and she wore her lion look, as Mother called it, all fierce about her love. Kinneret imagined Calev grinning, teeth white and dimples showing, as she took his arm during their Intended ceremony. In her head, she saw Oron braving the Pass's most powerful waves and expertly working the sails, once again saving her life and Avi's too.

"We are also good," she shouted into the air, defiance roaring through her heart.

But darkness trampled her memories and ground them into dust.

Runnos spoke. *You are mine.*

Her thoughts slid out of her mind like quick little fish, lost to the ocean of languid sensation and Runnos's dark, dark sway. The god ruled her. She loved him for it.

And she was very, very hungry.

One of those flames of life threw himself against a green man nearer to the pond. He moved like sunlight on wet leaves, unpredictable and quick. He struck the other green man's chest and face quickly enough not to be absorbed in any way.

Brave. That flame of life was brave like the familiar, most beautiful flame at her feet.

"Kinneret!" the familiar voice shouted. What was its name again? Ca...

She looked down to see him bleeding life onto the pine needles that had fallen from her tangled hair in the fight. She had broken him in some way she couldn't see. Not his body. His soul. His heart.

"Calev?" His name rose in her mind like the sun. She strained to understand what it meant. If only she could see his face instead of the blur of life that only looked like the sustenance she needed to satisfy this wild, gnawing hunger under every inch of her new flesh.

"Ona is nearly there. Just hold on to yourself a little longer. Please. Please."

No. Runnos was all she cared about. And feeding. What was this being saying? Why did she care? "Where?" Who was Ona? Her tongue was thick and didn't want to speak this language any more.

"The heart of the wood," the flickering life said. "She will end this suffering."

Runnos shrieked, and it was one thousand crows cawing, one thousand trees snapping in the wind, one thousand new trees bursting into life. Kinneret covered her ears and shrank from the sound, but the words drove straight into her mind like expertly aimed arrows.

Go to my grove. Under the pool. Absorb the woman's life.

"What is he telling you?" the little flame said. "Don't listen.

You are one of us. Not them. You don't have to listen to Runnos."

This being didn't understand. Runnos's orders were *in* her. She couldn't fight them just as she couldn't stop breathing. His demands were her demands.

Yes, the god whispered. That sweet warmth of Runnos's presence slid up her calves and over her ribs. The essence of him breathed into her neck, sending waves of heat down her body. The gnawing hunger ebbed away.

She sighed. This had to be the most wonderful feeling in the world.

With the hunger temporarily satiated, she opened her eyes. And saw the being's face. Every detail. His dark eyes. Ebony hair. The love in every feature.

Another green man grabbed the being and swung him into the air, snagged in fingerlike branches.

Kinneret snarled and lashed out at the other green man. "He is mine!"

She lashed out an arm like a whip of sinewy bark and ripped the small flame from her competition. He panted with fatigue and his fear-sweat rose from the coverings on his form.

She lodged him roughly onto her back as her roots rolled over the earth toward the pond.

"We can't go. Let Ona do her work. Please. Don't you remember?"

Runnos drove more orders like sharpened stone into Kinneret's mind. *Now. Destroy her. She is there, at my holy pine. Beyond the old sorcerer's barrier. The pond will not affect you in your form. Go. Dive. Now.*

The oddly familiar flame on her back grew quiet as her roots found the cool, silver pond. She couldn't remember why she had taken him like this. But there was some reason. It tickled her thoughts and she would let him be. Absorb him later.

"Green man." The flame on her back spoke in different tones now. He no longer seemed familiar. Now he frightened her. "The woman in the pond, in the hidden grove, she has a rune-etched sword that will end you if you try to stop her."

Kinneret paused, the silver pool lapping over the bark on her knees. She stared into the water's still depths. Tendrils of silver light danced below the surface.

Go. Now. Runnos sent a storm-scented wind across the pond. The air pulled Kinneret deeper. The orders forced her forward. All sound save Runnos's cooing voice faded as the pool's cloudy water welcomed Kinneret into its soft embrace. The hunger dimmed here, but Runnos's continued command of *Go. Now. Destroy.* pushed her onward.

The life on her back pressed into her shoulders, touched her cheek, then was gone. He had floated back to the surface. A part of her went with him, though she couldn't remember why he mattered so much. She would deal with that after ripping the woman flame apart.

The silvery water tugged at Kinneret's hair and the pine needles growing from the tips of each strand. Her powerful arms surged through the liquid and her roots grounded her, making each step long.

Runnos spoke quietly but firmly. *Keep on. Soon, you will reach the end of the barrier.*

And just as he said, the water began to give way to air at the tips of her roots. She stepped into the most sacred heart of the wood. Her new form grew jubilant at the sight of so many huge pines. The light here was like twilight, green and hazy from the barrier, but the trees didn't seem to suffer from the lack of sun. Something else fed them here. She leaned her mind into the shared thoughts of all the green men.

We feed them, the voices whispered.

By claiming the flames of life lured into the wood, the green men poured growth into this sacred place. Through roots and the very earth itself, Runnos's heart thrived.

The largest of the pines stood proud and dark at the base of a steep incline.

Beside it, a flame of life lifted something that gave off black curls of evil smoke.

It was the woman with the runed sword.

Kinneret sped down the slope, rage and fear rising behind Runnos's command.

Destroy.

ONA

From where Ona stood beside the pool, it looked as though Kinneret had grown even taller. She towered over Calev, who shouted her name. He was a fool for getting so close. She could crush him with one swing of a fist.

Ona was torn.

A huge part of her wanted to go after Miach, into the pool, to save him from those three green men who'd followed.

Another part of her had to stay here and fight with Dante and somehow help Calev shake Kinneret out of this change.

Kinneret whipped her branched arms toward Calev like she might grab for him. He slipped away, still calling out to her. The pain in his voice hurt her too. It was so raw and real. He was losing his essence here, now, as he lost the love of his life.

The wind gusted as Dante fought off another green man.

Pine needles and small branches like horns tangled in Kinneret's hair. She roared, the sound thundering through

Ona's bones. Now, she was the only one of Runnos's creatures present.

"Ona!" Dante waved a hand, then threw the runed sword in a high arc. "I name this sword Carver and give it to you freely."

The weapon bloomed into light briefly before landing blade first in the ground. Ona snatched it up. The hilt was still warm from Dante's hand. She lifted it, adjusting to the feel of its weight in her hand.

"Carver," she whispered. The runes on the blade flashed in response. She nearly dropped the sword. Northern witches called their staves by that name—carver—because of the blade each held at one end for making runes and drawing up magic.

"Go after Miach! I'll take care of them." Dante nodded at Calev and Kinneret.

Kinneret keened, her wail long and torturous. The sound buried itself in Ona's ringing ears.

Ona traded one last look with Dante, her heart snagging on a beat, then turned to that horrible silver water.

There was no time to worry about whether it would cause her intense pain like it had the first time she'd gone in. Kinneret was about to kill her own lover. Dante would be killed too. Oron was likely dead. And Miach and Ethus were being chased by three tree spirits.

No time for fear.

She simply had to be a warrior now.

There was no other choice.

The water was cool against her ripped clothing.

Sweat rolled down Ona's back, and she curled her spine like it might somehow protect her healing wounds from further injury.

Seren would've leapt right into the pool to save even one of her people. Ona could do this too.

The water slid past her elbows. A shiver rocked her hard.

Yes. Seren would've done this. Lucca too.

She focused on a memory of Lucca in battle. His ferocity and focus. The way he made certain to fight beside her.

Then Dante's face appeared in her mind's eye. He was also ferocious in a fight. But more reckless. More warrior. Less bookworm. Dante leaned on brute force more often than Lucca. But he was still intelligent.

Ona was surrounded by proud warriors of all kinds.

The water rose and swallowed her chin.

It passed over her mouth.

She could do this.

After all, Seren wasn't a warrior first and she handled the tough stuff fine. She was a ruler first. Ona didn't have to focus on the fighting all her life. Just right now. She could be an artist first, soldier second. That was doable.

The water rose over her nostrils.

She held her breath.

Her body shook. From fear? From pain? She wasn't certain.

The cold liquid pressed and touched and scratched against her.

Her eyes opened like they knew better than the rest of her that she'd have to see where she was heading. Feathery, sparkling water made up the whole of her view. She swam down, kicking her feet and keeping a firm hold on Carver.

Her lungs burned.

The water was endless.

She would die here, waiting for pain, striving to save them, longing to be the woman she knew she could be if given one more chance.

Then the water billowed away from her face. A valley opened up below. Great, green pines stretched wide, twisting limbs which cast strange, luminous shadows over a carpet of bluebells. Resin filled Ona's nose, and she gripped Carver in both hands.

The green men who'd chased Miach were moving at a fast clip down the slope that led into the valley.

High above them, Ona forced her legs to run.

Glimpses of Miach showed through the green men's limbs. He still held the shield over his head, and though he seemed to only be walking at a boy's pace, somehow he was far faster than the tree spirits. Maybe the shield was helping him. Maybe this place—sealed in a strange pool of magic the boy's own grandfather cast—recognized his blood and gave him an edge.

"I hope you give me an edge," she said to Carver.

The steel bit into the first green man's back like a fang, going deep. The tree spirit slumped. Ona yanked the sword from the woody flesh just before the thing tumbled down the incline. The second creature turned and howled, reaching for Carver. The weapon sizzled against the monster's hand. Ona twisted and lopped an arm completely off. The green man shrieked and came at her as the third creature joined him.

Ona backed up a step. There was no time for flint or spark, but a chant floated to the surface of her mind.

"I am the fox in the forest.
Clever and quick."

She spun and dragged Carver across the second green man's neck. Thick and pungent sap poured from the wound, but he kept coming.

"*I am the bird in the trees.*

Light as feathers."

Leaping, feeling the chant's power in her veins, she sprang over the third green man's shoulder.

"*I am the stag in the shadows.*

Crowned with power."

She bent Carver and drove its point into the green man's side. The blade ran clean through the creature so she rotated the steel, then ripped it back out, tearing the thing's insides apart.

Her stomach turned, but she faced the other tree spirit.

"For you, Lucca, so you'll meet your brother again. For you, Seren, because I want to deserve your friendship. For you, Miach, because I know what it is to lose so much. For you, Dante, because I owe you my life."

"*I am the bear.*

Clawed and unrelenting."

Muscles coiled and strength surging through her blood, she jumped and flipped the sword.

"*Wake, iron, wake!*"

Carver blazed white as she gripped it in both hands and forced the runed steel into the last green man.

The tree spirit dissolved into a cloud of green-black mist.

She exhaled in a gust of air, arms shaking.

Below, Miach and Ethus marched toward the largest of all the pines. Its branches stretched slowly, menacingly, toward him.

Getting her feet under her, Ona started down the hill. "Miach! It's alive. Stay back!"

The ground evened out and Ona jumped over a boulder, then launched herself over a small stream.

"Miach!"

The tree nearly had him.

Under Ona's boots, the ground vibrated.

Voices scattered in the valley's wind.

Rise. Defend.

It was the voice of Runnos and his green men.

Miach turned as Ona ran up to him. "This is the sacred pine," he said. "You know what to do."

There was a glow to Miach's eyes that showed the centuries of his existence.

"Miach, come. We must get away from here." She grabbed his arm, but he held firmly to his spot, shield still raised, as the tree's branches creaked and lowered toward them.

"Use my father's sword."

"Carver."

Miach laughed. He actually laughed, and they were about to die. "That is a perfect name."

"What? What do you mean? Come, let's go."

"You are an artist. Make your mark on the tree."

"My mark?"

He took one hand from the shield to touch a rune on Carver's shining blade. "Like those. Close your eyes. Let my grandfather's magic speak to you."

What was he talking about? "Your grandfather lost the battle against Runnos long ago."

"Did he?" That ancient glow in Miach's eyes brightened. "Sometimes the war lasts longer than one man's life."

Goosebumps flew down Ona's arms.

This wasn't just Miach she was talking to. This was his grandfather. The great sorcerer.

Miach rose onto the tips of his toes to hold the shield over them both.

Ona poised the tip of Carver's steel against the huge pine.

The tree froze.

A gust of chill wind blasted Ona's back. Carver slipped from her hand and fell to the ground.

"Ona!" Miach's voice was all boy now. "It's Kinneret! Hurry!"

The fierce kaptan and salt witch had fully morphed into a green man.

Dark emerald green—almost black—cloaked the entire expanse of her eyes, whites and all. Every finger ended in jagged branches, some with pine needles and others with vines tinged in blood red. Her cheekbones and chin had sharpened into vicious edges, distorting her beauty into terror. Two great vines of black and red and green snapped from her back like wings. She used them to grab boulders and earth as she rushed toward Ona and Miach.

Ona had thought she'd known fear.

When the Invaders came to her home and killed her aunt. Then, on the battlefield at Akhayma, when the Invader ran her through and life bled out of her.

But this was a fresh fear.

Kinneret was an angel of horror Ona had never expected or imagined. Soldiers killed with sword, arrow, fist, or spear. She had no idea how this bent creature—woven out of a new friend and a curse—would bring death.

Knees quaking, Ona knelt and grasped for Carver. Her fingers closed around pine needles and dirt wedged itself under her nails.

"The sword. I need the sword."

Miach held the shield upright, arms shaking. "I can't let the shield go. He'll take us even before she does." His gaze flicked to the great pine that had begun to stretch down and bend over them.

Ona found Carver, then did the most difficult thing she'd ever done.

She turned her back on the threat and let the artist in her take over.

Drawing the bright blade over the pine's trunk, she carved a slanted line. Her wrist turned, aching, and she created another line that crossed the first.

"Ona!" Miach bumped against her, Ethus at their feet.

She could feel Kinneret's power at her back and the force of the pine burning in the air all around them.

Carver moved so easily against Runnos's pine. The runes blazed moon-white.

A voice echoed in Ona's ears.

Stop them.

Pain shot through her head and ricocheted down her body. Her battle wound pulsed. She bit her lip to keep from crying out as the heat of new blood leaked from her side and her shoulder. It was the curse again. She kept hold of the sword though. She didn't lose it. Not yet.

Destroy. Destroy. Destroy.

Ona brought Carver's hilt high. One last mark. The sword's power shivered into Ona's arms. Tilting the blade a fraction, she placed the tip under the tree's flesh, then drove the steel down. The pine roared. The last mark became a clean swathe of silver.

The valley shook, leaves dropped to the earth, and roots tore themselves from the dirt. Kinneret shrieked, her arms flailing.

The watery sky—the sorcerer's spell—exploded into a flood of sparkling rain.

Miach shouted something, grinning, and gripped the shield to his chest. "Farewell, Ona! I see them and I'm going to them now!"

Ona blinked. "Miach?"

The solidity of his face, arms, and legs began to fade. Ethus was disappearing too.

Kinneret ran her palms over her head and raised her face to smile. No pine needles showed in her hair or along her eyelashes. The branches that had protruded from her skull and back fell to her feet. She touched her arm tentatively as the flesh resumed its original light brown hue.

Ona ran to her and clasped Kinneret's human fingers in her own. "You're back, Kaptan."

Kinneret's joyful look dissolved into one of horror. She twisted away to run up the hill, out of the valley. "Calev!"

Ona turned to see not Miach or Ethus, but only the shield. It sat quietly beside the great pine. Runnos's pine. She bent to touch the quartz stone on the shield. "Be well, Miach. Be well. Ethus, you take care of him, all right?"

Sunlight warmed Ona's left side as she stood. The rune she'd carved into the great pine glowed lightly. The tree was just a tree now. The air around it was simply forest air. None of the foul power of a bent god tainted its presence any longer.

With the immediate danger gone, Ona had one thought.

Dante.

Carver in hand, she sprinted up the hill, marveling at how her wounds no longer pulsed in pain. They were not completely healed, but not far from it.

Out of the valley, Kinneret and Dante bent their heads over

Calev. He sat up and Kinneret pulled him against her. Dante's chin lifted and he saw Ona.

Ona ran to him, but once she was there, against his chest, breathing, she didn't know exactly what to say. *I just saved the day. Thank you for the fabulous sword. I really need a nap. That adorable boy and his goat passed on to their family and I don't quite know how. I forgot to pick up the shield.*

Dante raised his eyebrows. "You look like you're about to explode."

"I am. Are you all right?" She ran hands over his arms and chest, forgetting for a moment that they hardly knew one another.

He covered her hands with his. "I am."

"That was...madness."

"I'm sure. Where is Miach?"

"He disappeared. Ethus too. Miach told me he was going to them. I can only guess he meant he was passing on to be with his family."

Dante exhaled slowly.

Ona stuck the sword into his belt. "You're certain you're all right?"

"Yes," a different voice said. "I am all right, and thank you so much for asking!" Oron walked up to Kinneret and tapped her on the shoulder.

The kaptan shrieked, this time in delight. Ona grinned as Kinneret and Calev embraced the man. They looked like a family and it made Ona miss Lucca terribly.

"Glad you're not a tree!" Dante saluted Oron, then put his hands on Ona's shoulders gently. "What exactly happened down there?"

The silver pool was of course gone. The whole area had

obviously been spelled to look smaller than it was. The valley undulated far beyond where the pool had been. It made Ona a little dizzy.

"It's a long story. How about I tell you on the way to Akhayma?"

"To see Lucca."

"Of course."

"He might hate me."

"That makes two of us. We're going anyway."

"I suppose we are. What is that saying you and my brother have? Your wishes are my wishes?"

"As long as yours don't war with mine." Ona touched the corner of Dante's sly grin and wished she wasn't as tired as the dead.

22

KINNERET

Kinneret lifted her tear-stained face from Calev's tunic, then she kissed him. He obviously wasn't angry with her for losing her part of the battle with Runnos, because he gripped her hips and pressed hard into the kiss. His breath was warm, and he smelled like he always did, like sun-warmed earth and lemons. Lord of the Harvest. And he was hers. Her body heated against his and she dug her fingers into the waves of his ebony hair.

"Kinneret." He spoke into her neck, mouth pressed against her sticky skin.

Thankfully, it seemed that Ona and Dante were busy talking a bit of a ways off.

Then there was a voice. And a tapping on her shoulder.

"Oron!" In her excitement, Kinneret shoved Calev away, but Calev laughed it off. She gripped Oron's wide face in her hands. "I am so angry with you."

"I just escaped a tree. You aren't allowed to be mad."

Her hands went to her hips. "Well, I am. You drank too much. You let your anger take you."

"Fine. You're permitted one full day of being angry with me."

"Good." Dante shouted something at Oron, but Kinneret didn't hear it. She was lost, staring at Oron and thanking Fire and sea that he was alive.

"Ona!" she called. "We need to hear what happened under the water. But first, let's get back to the road and try to rummage up some food and drink."

"I do like your priorities, Kinneret," Oron said.

A shout of greeting came from the trees. Then another. Another.

A group of five men and two women filtered into the small clearing.

"What happened?" a woman in a light-colored dress asked in the trade tongue.

Two men walked beside her, talking to one another in quick Silvanian. The first wore noble livery and the second had a beard far too large for his face.

All of them had dirt on their faces and leaves on their clothing or in their hair. The woman was missing one shoe.

Oron swallowed loudly. "I think these might be people who were also trapped by the green men."

Calev stood slowly. "Maybe these are the people taken recently whose spirits had not yet been fully absorbed by the wood."

Kinneret wasn't sure what to say. "Welcome. Our friend Ona here," she gestured to the mercenary, "somehow stopped the forest god and freed you. At least, that's what I know."

"That's about it," Ona said. "I used the runed sword to bind Runnos."

The man in noble livery scratched his head. "I feel like I've been dreaming for a month."

"More like having a nightmare, wasn't it?" Oron asked.

"Yes."

"We'd offer you food and water, but we have none," Dante said.

"Thank you," the woman said. "I am Rosa. This is my friend Giuseppe." She pointed to the man in the livery. "I'd love to hear how you managed to defeat a god, but I just want to get back to my family in Verita."

"Of course!" Kinneret said. "Travel with us. We're headed there too. We have a meeting with the king."

"Oh!" Giuseppe clapped his long hands. "We work for a member of his court."

The rest of the freed people greeted Ona and thanked her before hurrying out of the forest in pairs. Finally, Kinneret and the rest gathered themselves and did the same.

As they walked, headed for the charcoal burners' huts to beg some food and a night's rest, Kinneret talked in whispers with Ona and Oron. The horror of Runnos had personally touched each one and Kinneret was relieved to have two people who— at least a little bit—understood. Dante and Calev let them have their restorative conversations, almost serving as guards along the road, Dante with the sword he had named Carver, and Calev with his dagger and keen eyes. Rosa and Giuseppe kept their own company, talking in serious tones nearby.

At a rippling stream, the group stopped and washed the

cursed forest off of them. Blood, leaves, magic, and tears. All of it. With no dry clothing to change into, Kinneret shivered a little in the breeze as she took up her discussions of Runnos, the sorcerer, Miach, and the green men with Oron and Ona.

"So Miach's grandfather was actually the reason why Miach was still alive."

Ona tied her hair up into two knots. "Yes, but Runnos twisted the magic and used Miach for his own purposes."

Oron frowned. "But how did the spell get to Miach when the man died before he was born?"

"That, I don't know." Ona shrugged. "Magic?"

"Indeed," Oron said wryly.

"And when you were in the silver pool, Miach took on some of his grandfather's spirit?"

"It looked like that to me," Ona said. "His eyes were… different. Old. Powerful. He showed me a rune to carve into the sacred pine. It was on Carver's blade."

Kinneret was overwhelmed. "I can't help but think you were…destined for the job of taking Runnos down. I mean, you are a warrior and an artist. It's like it was all fated."

"Just as you are a fabulously talented sailor with a fierce heart, determined to get rich, and you found Ayarazi," Oron said.

"It wasn't just about the silver," Kinneret said, "and you know it."

"I do." Oron patted Kinneret's arm.

"It must've been amazing to see the silver pool from below and watch it blow apart."

Ona nodded. "It was. I've seen a lot of things, but that beat them all. You were there, but I suppose you don't remember."

"I don't." Shame heated Kinneret's throat.

"Kinneret." Ona's earnest eyes caught her gaze. "Don't do that. Don't blame yourself. I'm guessing you held out against Runnos's magic far longer than any of us could have."

"Agreed," Oron said. "And from what I've heard, we should be glad Dante didn't lop your head off with that fine, new sword. He is quite the swordsman, hmm?"

Kinneret knew he was trying to change the subject. "I hurt everyone. Most of all, Calev."

Calev walked ahead with Dante. He pulled his dagger and showed Dante the hilt. He was probably telling Dante all the Old Farm legends about the Dagger Dance. Kinneret wanted to be happy, but she only felt really, really sorry about losing her mind in the forest.

Ona's gaze brightened. "Kinneret." The former mercenary's eyebrows flew together in a vicious scowl. "No, you didn't hurt everyone. Runnos did. And we took his tail down. So just stop with the whole *I'm terrible* thing. You aren't and we know it and you know it. You are amazing." She punched Kinneret lightly on the arm.

Kinneret had to smile. "I think I like you."

"I know I like you."

"I'm in love with you both. In an older brother kind of way, that is." Oron hugged them briefly. "Thanks for not leaving me in the tree."

"Avi would've killed me if I had," Kinneret said.

Oron laughed the first real laugh since they were on Ekrem's full-ship. "I will be sure to write her a fine thank you note for her murderous reputation upon our return."

AFTER WHAT FELT like a short journey and a terribly long one combined somehow, Kinneret looked up from Oron's and Ona's faces to see the charcoal burner, who'd let Calev and her rest, coming out to greet them.

The woman raised her hands. "You survived it. I hardly believe my own eyes. And you got your friends with you too. This is a cause for celebration. Hardy, get those eggs you found in the treeline last night. We're having a feast."

It was no feast, but the eggs were very, very good.

The charcoal burner, named Valentina, had talked her fellows into dragging two stumps and a wooden plank in front of her hut. The whole group sat down to fresh water, pine needle tea, and plates of eggs and greens.

"Thank you, Valentina," Kinneret said to the woman.

Valentina handed the bowl of eggs to a woman sitting across the basic plank table. "No. Thank *you*!"

"For what?"

"You set the cursed wood to rights, didn't you?"

"We did," Ona said. Her voice was stronger than it had been since Kinneret met the mercenary. And there was a lightness to her walk despite the sadness that still reigned in her eyes. "Runnos is bound now."

Oron rubbed the back of his neck. He'd shown Kinneret the red marks left by the tree's first grab at him. "That wood is still not the most pleasant spot."

Ona smiled a little. "No. But I think..." She glanced at Carver. Dante had given the sword back to her, saying Miach would've wanted her to have it. "I think he can only scare people a bit now. He can't do anything too horrible."

Oron snorted. "So maybe just some creepy whispering and the occasional tree with a trunk that just sort of resembles a man?"

"Yes. Maybe just that. Probably less than that."

Valentina didn't seem to understand they were joking. "The animals are back. That's what I have seen. The rabbits bothered my garden again today. The deer ran across the road. Things are the way they are supposed to be again. Like they were when my mother's mother was a child."

Dante swallowed a bite of egg, then pointed to a spot between two beech trees. "You should plant some of that woody herb that's growing right there in your garden. Might dissuade the rabbits a little. Not completely. But a little."

Ona shook her head. "Why is it that I'm the one who actually lived in a forest for years with your brother and you're the one who knows all about plants?"

"Guess you were focused on something else during those years."

"I was."

Kinneret wished her younger years could've focused on something other than starving. "And you had someone else to find dinner for you."

Ona had the decency to look abashed. "I did. I was fortunate. The mercenaries I fought with had a cook. She was very good."

"You're a mercenary?" Valentina didn't look happy about the fact.

"I was. Not anymore."

Valentina breathed out and passed some field greens to the charcoal burner next to her at the table. "Good. I didn't think you had the eyes of a killer."

"I have killed many." Ona didn't look proud.

"But you won't anymore. You are something else." Valentina tapped her chin and studied Ona. "Maybe a scribe?

You sound learned and your hands look very capable of delicate things."

Ona held them up. "They do?"

Valentina elbowed Dante and winked. "They surely do. Don't they, handsome?"

Dante looked like he'd just been smacked with an oar. "Uh, yes." He grinned and chuckled.

Kinneret could've stayed here for three days instead of one night. Valentina and the rest of her crew were full of laughs and good sense. Kinneret didn't realize she'd miss the humility of spending time with the low-caste type. Well, Valentina would be considered low-caste here in Silvania although the Empire's caste system held no sway here. Silvania still had one. It was simply invisible. Lately, Kinneret had spent most of her non-sailing sun at Amir Ekrem's little court, surrounded by the haughty and the overly educated.

"Eh, Calev." She nudged him with her foot, and he eyed her behind his cup of pine needle tea. "After we marry, can we spend our month going from port to port, down the coast? I need more real folk in my life and fewer highly educated knob-heads."

Calev sputtered, then laughed. "Sounds great to me. First, we have to survive the Silvanian king's court."

Kinneret sighed. "I'm definitely going to need some new clothes." One of her capped sleeves hung limply over her shoulder and a tear ran from the hem of her skirt all the way to her knee. And some of the dirt from the forest didn't come out when they'd washed in the stream.

Across the table, Oron lifted a hand. "Spending silver is one of my greatest joys. I will be happy to help."

"You're hired." She suddenly missed the presence of Miach and Ethus. The moon rose over the road and the charcoal pits. The white light washed over everyone's faces, making them look like ghosts. "I wonder how disappearing felt to Miach and Ethus."

Calev stared at the moon too. "Ona said he was smiling. I'd guess it was better than we can imagine. He'd been lonely for too long."

The urge to kiss Calev's cheek overwhelmed her and she leaned in close. His skin was warm. His growing beard pricked her lips.

"What was that for?" he asked.

"For being you." She gave him one more peck on the cheek, then turned to Rosa and Giuseppe. "Do you work for a noble family then?"

"We do," Rosa said. "And I have an idea. I think you should keep your torn clothing, as we will. We will go right into the court as is, and you can tell the whole story. You and yours here saved our country, if not the entire continent. The king must acknowledge that feat and surely he'll agree to whatever you demand."

Ona leaned in. "I like the sound of that. Dante and I need horses for our trip to Akhayma. Silver would help too."

"I do need to eat." Dante patted his flat stomach.

Oron nodded appreciatively over a heaping forkful of egg.

"I wouldn't want to return Lucca's brother in a state of emaciation," Ona said.

"Of what?" Valentina asked.

"It means he'd be missing all those muscles of his." Ona poked at Dante's big arm appreciatively.

Grinning, Kinneret wondered how long it would be until

those two traded more than jokes. Two days on the road. That was her private bet.

When Kinneret and the rest were full of eggs, exhaustion caught up and dragged them all into a deep sleep.

Kinneret dreamed of Miach and Ethus.

23

ONA

Verita blew Ona's hair back. Yes, she was from Silvania, but she'd never gone to the huge port city to see its ornate merchant houses or streets of water where traders rode boats more often than horses. It was a city of islands. And silver. The wealth dripped off the nobility here. Ona and her group did not belong. At all. In torn trousers, tattered shirts, and muddied tunics, they didn't look like they should be approaching the king's castle.

Kinneret had retrieved a harried-looking woman named Ridhima from the dock. She had been guarding the skiff Kinneret came in on. After a quick tale about what had happened and assurances that all was well for the time being, they sent Ridhima off to give word to their full-ship crew about the delay.

At the king's castle, a young woman with black and silver hair strolled out of the archway. A group came up alongside her. She held a bladed staff and inclined her head to Calev, Kinneret, and Oron.

"You retrieved your friend," the woman said. She must've been from the Northern Isles.

"Yes," Calev said. "Thank you for your help."

Oron was stiff, but he nodded a thank you. "I heard you told my friends about my unfortunate situation. I appreciate your break from tradition. Maybe you can enlighten the rest of Snowfallen when you return."

She frowned and studied him. Her group left without a backward glance. "Perhaps," the woman said. Tucking her fine cloak around her, she swept into the road beside the canal.

Ona touched Carver's hilt. "I should've asked her about the runes."

"I can tell you a little," Oron said. "I was born in the isles."

Rosa and Giuseppe greeted the guards outside the arched walls. "We are of the DeLuca household," Giuseppe said in quick Silvanian. He gestured to his mucked-up livery. The silver embroidery and fine fabric didn't match his unshaved chin and blackened eye.

The guards scowled. "Is Master DeLuca expecting you at court? Like this?" one of them asked.

Rosa smiled, indulgent. "We have a great story to tell the king. It will please him. If not, you will have the pleasure of kicking us into the canal."

The guards laughed and waved the group on.

Inside the first gate, a courtyard bustled with boys saddling horses the color of night and gondolas bumping out of a tunnel and up to a dock. Strips of rainbow-colored fabric streamed from the dock's silver-painted poles. Dodging a spirited gelding that Ona wished she could ride to Akhayma, they came to a second set of guards standing at an arched doorway. Voices echoed from the high entrance.

Rosa gave these guards a similar treatment.

"What if the king decides he isn't wild about seven beggars barging into his throne room?" Ona's palms began to sweat. She wished she was on the road, heading toward Lucca and Seren already.

"Then we'll have another night of sleep. Perhaps in a prison cell." Dante shrugged.

"Great."

A hallway of mirrors and windows threw spears of light onto a ceiling covered in detailed paintings.

"I might actually be fine with a night in prison," Oron said. "I'm a walking corpse right now."

As she studied the shape of a painted rock dove above their heads, Ona threw an arm around Oron. "Maybe you can steal a nobleman's wine?" Her fingers itched to paint a better version of that bird on the room's elaborate ceiling.

"If one thing could bring me back to life, that would be it."

"It'd have to be a good red, though, right?" Dante looked very serious.

"Definitely," Oron said. "Bring up my part of the tale right at the beginning of our audience with the king, Ona. Then I'll have a little sun to harvest an unattended glass."

"Can do."

The king of Silvania stood with his back to a massive, silver throne. He laughed—a deep and bellowing sound—before turning around to see what the cat had dragged in.

The servant at the door announced them. "Two of the DeLuca household bring you a tale they believe will entertain the court, your highness.

Ona had told Rosa and Giuseppe everything she could remember from the time in the cursed wood, but they hadn't practiced for this, and Ona wasn't sure if she was supposed to speak up or not.

The king tilted his head to one side. "Hmm. That sounds interesting. Ah. Is that Kaptan Kinneret Raza and Calev ben Y'hoshua I see there?"

Kinneret and Calev bowed.

"I thought we were set to speak yesterday morning. Or was it the day before that? I'm not accustomed to being ignored."

Calev stammered and Kinneret stepped forward. "Your highness, we apologize for the inconvenience. You see, a group of drunken sailors—not mine—stole a friend of ours away and he ended up in a cursed forest not far from Verita. So you'll excuse us, please, if our near death experience made us late for a meeting."

Calev grimaced and took over, hands clasped. "Your highness. This is the story we are here to tell. Please forgive us for causing you any inconvenience."

"And for looking like beggars in your gorgeous court, your highness," Oron said. "I will happily start the tale. A glass of wine might help me speak more clearly."

The king's frown smoothed, and he laughed. Clapping his hands, he said, "Give them food and drink. Then, when they are fully ready, this good man can start the telling."

Oron gave a ridiculously low bow, but the king chuckled, obviously enjoying the expert sailor's whimsical way. If Lucca had been here, he'd have loved Oron. Ona wanted to ask him to come with them to Akhayma, but there was no way he'd leave his job with Kinneret.

Oron downed a glass in what seemed like one swallow. He

cleared his throat. "It all began when an innocent and rather intelligent fellow went for a drink not far from here. Yes, he most likely had too many..."

The tale went on and on.

The king and his court gasped and laughed at all the right spots. Ona spilled her end of the story and brought out Carver for all to gawk over.

The king touched the blade. "May I?"

Ona nodded, and the king took the hilt and lifted the sword. He moved well enough—a respectable swordsman if not a little overdramatic with his striking. A lady in red velvet squeaked as the king swept the sharp edge close to her feet. His laughter was infectious though and soon she was joining in.

The telling was over.

Ona needed the king to give her horses and coin. Without it, she'd have to beg off Kinneret and Calev, who had stores on their full-ship. She really didn't want to do that.

"Your highness, did you enjoy the story?"

"I did." He gently handed Carver to her. "This has been the most entertainment we've had since my old jester decided he'd had enough of me!"

The court erupted over what Ona assumed was some sort of inside joke.

"Would you consider a...reward for such a tale?" Ona swallowed, watching the king take a glass of red wine back to his throne.

He stopped, then turned on his heel. "I would! Just tell me what you need, and it will be given to you."

Ona exhaled, relief flooding her. "Two horses. For me and for Dante." She gestured toward Dante, who bowed roughly.

"And perhaps a small sum so we may eat and drink during our journey to Akhayma."

"Why do you head to the Empire's capitol?"

"I have a message for the new kyros."

"I heard she is a beauty."

"She is very powerful. The Fire blesses her with visions."

"I will have to be careful then when we meet for negotiations."

Calev and Kinneret stepped forward. "Speaking of negotiations, Amir Ekrem worries that Invaders may come around the southern tip of the continent and attack Jakobden's ports."

"He believes they are capable of doing so much by sea?" the king asked. "They are more of a land army, aren't they? The new kyros destroyed the bulk of that army, did she not?"

"That's the message we received," Calev said. "But there are wanderers. Invaders who have broken from the main force and now travel the countryside pillaging."

The king set his wine on a small, round table. "I can see how that would pose a threat to Jakobden's trade."

"And a threat to those lemons you love," Calev added.

The king arranged his sumptuous clothing around his large body and sat on the silver throne. "I would hate to miss out on that taste." He held up the fingers of his right hand and kissed them loudly. "So delicious! Now, what exactly does Amir Ekrem want from me?"

"If we are raided by Invaders and have at least three witnesses to the event, Amir Ekrem asks that you send two full-ships. Armed. And three smaller vessels to the Pass to stand in defense of the area for one moon cycle. After that, Amir Ekrem will renegotiate with you."

"Agreed."

"You are?" Kinneret's eyes were wide.

Ona snorted. "The man knows what he wants. A true Silvanian," she whispered.

Kinneret whistled low. "Well, then we are agreed."

The king ordered his servants to hand out more wine in celebration and demanded that everyone dance. A flute player began piping and a man with a huge oud strummed his strings vigorously. A boy from the stables was summoned to ready horses and packs for Ona and Dante.

Ona smiled. It was great to hear Silvanian music again.

Kinneret turned to Calev. "Will you dance with me, my love?"

Ona left them to it and found Dante. "Should we try to leave now?"

"Why not have a bit of fun first?" Dante held out a hand and wiggled his eyebrows at the musicians.

Ona took his offered hand and put it on her hip. "Let's see what you've got, big man."

24

ONA

Nearly One Year Later

As Ona rode beside Dante, toward the great walls of Akhayma, she realized that, in her mind, this city hadn't changed in almost a year. She'd frozen the place in time, fully expecting to see pillars of blue-black smoke like mournful ghosts all around the battlefield. Seren would've ordered the people to burn bodies of the Invaders as well as those of fallen Empire soldiers. The air should've been rank with flame and flesh. But that had all happened months and months ago.

Back in Verita, right after the battle with Runnos, Dante and Ona both had run into relatives in the port city.

With the happy reunions, they'd been talked into waiting to return until now.

Ona hadn't fought her cousin's request that she stay because she'd been afraid still, afraid she'd be turned away at Akhayma, afraid her heart and Dante's would be broken by Lucca and Seren.

But there could be no more stalling.

A year. It was far too long already. Seren would've already held another Fire Ceremony as kyros. They'd have long since forgotten about Ona, but she owed them a sincere apology and an explanation and they would have it.

Dante hadn't argued against staying in Verita either. He hadn't even brought up the idea that they send a message to his brother. She recognized her own fear of rejection in his eyes.

So they'd had drinks and visited with cousins and enjoyed the king's continued good will through several moon cycles of gondolas and late nights talking about what their lives might look like now.

That's how they ended up arriving at Akhayma, not right after the battle with the Invaders, but long past that and nearly time for the Gathering.

Soon, people from all over Seren's Empire would descend onto the plains, raise luxurious tents, and compete in a number of archery, racing, and strategy tests for bragging rights—at least that's how Kinneret had explained it before she'd returned to Jakobden with Calev and Oron.

"Do you think they truly believe you're dead?" Dante clicked his tongue at his black gelding and the horse hurried into a trot.

Ona nudged her mount with a bump from her heels. "Yes." What would they say? Would they be happy to see her or horrified?

The horses' hooves kicked up clouds of the sandy earth as they made their way to the front gate. Ona had made this trip with Lucca once. She remembered her awe at the honeycomb structure of the gate and the colors of the stone walls. They were still impressive. She would paint them. Soon. Now, she was the artist she'd never let herself be. Even if she hadn't created a thing yet. It was in her, the artwork. It beat inside her chest like a second heart.

The guards stopped them, their acorn-shaped helmets shining. Rings of gray hung below the men's eyes. This had to have been one of the worst years in the city's history. So much loss.

"Kyros Seren will want to see me," Ona said. "I have news from the king of Silvania."

The first guard called in a few others, and the group escorted Ona and Dante toward the Kyros Walls, inside the city proper.

THE MAIN TENT looked much the same as it had before the battle. Beautiful stars of pale gossamer in the ceiling. Oil lamps, shined to a glow, hanging from the dark, peaked fabric of the tent. Tables lining the walls and one raised table at the end of the room.

And there was Seren.

Dante mimicked Ona as she chewed her provided mint leaf obediently, passed a hand over the Holy Fire bowl, then approached Seren.

"Kyros." Ona's voice faltered.

Seren stood. Her ebony hair fell over her shoulder, and the green cosmetics on her eyes twinkled. Her mouth opened. Shut. Opened again. "Ona?"

Ona nodded. "I am so sorry." She dropped to her knees.

Seren hurried around the table, face unreadable. Was she

going to hit Ona? Order her to a grisly death? Neither would surprise Ona.

But Seren took Ona's hands in hers. "Stand," the kyros said in Silvanian.

Ona did. She gripped Seren's fingers, afraid that if she let go, she'd never see this new friend again.

Seren blinked. "I can hardly believe it," she said, this time using the trade tongue. Her smile was radiant. "I thought you…I thought you were a ghost."

Dante stayed back, near the door with the guards who were watching closely.

"I felt like I was dead. An Invader ran me through on the battlefield. The only thing that kept me alive was the possibility of apologizing to you. I'm sorry for betraying you, my friend. I will never, ever do it again. Not that I expect you to trust me."

"Why did you go to Varol's side? I have my guesses, but…"

"Because I thought his kind of leadership would win against the Invaders. I thought you were too soft." Ona hated the words, but she had to be completely honest out of respect for Seren.

Seren closed her eyes briefly, and a sad smile crossed over her mouth. "You needed your revenge. For your aunt."

"But that's just it. Even after I killed so many Invaders. Even now, knowing we won against them and you annihilated their army—the feeling didn't satisfy me. All the death hollowed me out. I was a husk. It confused me. I didn't know who I was without that need to avenge my aunt's death."

Ona told Seren everything. About Runnos and Kinneret. About Dante.

"You are Ona the artist," Seren said.

Ona's smile was unstoppable. "I am."

A man emerged from the back door. Curly, black hair. Dark eyes. A walk like a lion.

"Lucca!" Ona threw herself at him.

His breath gusted out as he caught her. "Ona?"

She didn't want to look up from his shoulder, to break the embrace, to see if he was happy or upset by her arrival. She breathed him in, feeling safe and purely happy.

Then his chest heaved. His arms squeezed her tightly. "My friend. My Ona."

Wake. Her aunt's voice, the sound she'd heard on the battlefield the day she'd thought she'd died, echoed in her mind again. Finally, she understood. Her aunt had wanted her to wake from the nightmare of vengeance so Ona could enjoy life again. *Wake.*

I've done it, Aunt, she whispered.

Ona and Lucca didn't say another thing. They just cried and held one another until the storm passed.

When it did, Dante came forward, out of the shadows. "Brother."

Ona broke from Lucca and wiped her face with her sleeve. "I brought you a gift."

"No." Lucca shook his head, his eyes red. "No."

Dante smiled tentatively. "Yes. And I have forgiveness to ask too. I...I never thought our father would treat you or mother badly when I left. He hated me. I had to leave. Please know I wouldn't do it again. If I could go back and change my actions, I would. Now. Immediately. But I was—"

Lucca turned away and cleared his throat. Dante's hands fisted at his sides. He looked miserable.

"You were young," Lucca said. "You were hurt. You thought it was best at the time." His voice was raspy with emotion, and

Ona's heart bled for the child he was when his older brother ran away. "There is nothing to forgive," he whispered.

Dante shook his head in disagreement. "When I crossed out of Silvania, near the Green Mountains, a band of Invaders captured me. They trained me as their own. I fought here. In Akhayma. Out there." He jabbed a finger toward the door. "On that battlefield. And I'm sorry. I didn't want to," he said to Seren, "if that's any consolation. I accept whatever punishment you see fit."

"There will be no punishment," Seren said regally. "I too was assaulted by Invaders. I know well what they do to children and families. I will not punish you for simply staying alive and doing what you had to do."

Lucca walked toward Dante. "Brother."

Dante gripped Lucca's forearm. "Brother."

They hugged one another and whispered phrases touched by tears.

Ona's body was light as a feather. She'd done it. She was redeemed.

25
KINNERET

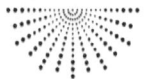

Akhayma's plains held an ocean of tents that rippled in the breeze. Kinneret slipped inside the first of Old Farm's clutch of tents, a green creation that was more of an oak's color than a pine's, which was a very good thing considering her past.

The cloth door adjoining this tent to the next fluttered. Someone was coming.

Please don't be Calev's Aunt Y'hudit, Kinneret thought. The woman was kind, but she was a lot to take in the morning.

But the nosy woman who'd jokingly hounded Kinneret about her first nights as Calev's wife didn't walk through the door. It was Calev himself.

Her heart swelled and she opened her arms.

Calev lifted her and swung her around, burying his face in her hair. "Are you going to compete today?"

Kinneret kissed him, savoring the taste of lemon on his warm lips and loving the feel of his strong arms. She pulled away, and his big, dark eyes opened. His lashes were ridiculously long.

"In the archery contest?" she said. "I'm not nearly good enough to go up against the people here."

"Come on. It'll still be exciting. The kyros herself is competing."

"I can't *wait* to see that. After the stories Ona told about that woman on horseback… If I compete, you have to as well. You're no slouch with a bow. Plus, I'd like to see you up there, in front of the crowd, knowing you're mine."

"You want to show off your new husband, do you?" Calev's hand snaked under the hem of her shirt. His fingers dragged lightly across her ribs.

She shivered. "Definitely." Her body fit against his perfectly. Like he was made for her. His hipbones pressed gently into her and she curled her fingers in his wavy hair.

With one last kiss, she pulled him out of the tent to find Avi, who was supposedly about to meet her friend Radi, a native to this area. They'd been exchanging letters for a long while.

"Avi!" Kinneret kept Calev's calloused fingers in hers as they wove through the Old Farm camp, toward Amir Ekrem's camp.

In the center of three blue tents—a makeshift courtyard of sorts—Avi sat across a gaming board from the boy Kinneret could only guess was Radi. He moved a glass game piece, then Avi laughed. She moved another piece. "I think you let me win."

"I did not," Radi said, appearing insulted. "I would never! I am simply gathering information about how you play. Next time, or perhaps the game after that, I will be the victor."

"We'll see." Avi raised an eyebrow. Then she noticed Kinneret and Calev and stood in one graceful movement. "Sister! Brother! Come meet Radi."

Radi gave them a simple bow. "Your sister has been busy annihilating me on the game board."

"I'll teach you how to best her," Calev said.

Avi stuck her tongue out at him like she was still a child.

Heart warm, Kinneret laughed, then hugged Avi and kissed her sun-colored braid. "Where is Oron?"

"I am here, my lady." The man himself walked out from the pathway between two tents, wine in hand. He lifted it high. "I have a surprise for you!" He turned and held out a palm.

Dante and another man who looked a great deal like Dante walked into the courtyard.

"Greetings!" Dante said. "This is my brother Lucca, the famous mercenary."

"I've heard so much about you all," Lucca said. He embraced each of them like they were kin, Kinneret last. "Thank you," he said sincerely. "Thank you for bringing my brother and my friend, Ona, back to me. Back to life. It is a miracle. I was told what you lived through and how you fought. I am in your debt."

Kinneret's cheeks were hurting from smiling so much. Where was Aunt Y'hudit when you needed to frown? "No, there is no debt," she said. "Ona is the hero. She saved us all, she and Miach."

Miach and his sorcerer grandfather often visited Kinneret's dreams. She often wondered what parts of the dreams were real and what were merely her own inventions.

"Oron, how did you find Dante?" Calev set up the gaming board, his fingers quick on the shining glass pieces.

"Once you've fought a forest together, you have a special kind of link. And before you say anything disparaging about my lazing about a tree trunk whilst you all raised sword and shield,

I'll have you know that battles are not always fought and won with the physical body."

"I wouldn't dream of disparaging you, Oron. And I heartily agree." Kinneret shuddered, remembering the feel of Runnos's voice inside her head. Her nightmares brought the god back to full power at least once a moon cycle. She longed to see Ona, the woman who'd fought by her side during that terrible time in the cursed forest. Somehow, Kinneret thought maybe seeing Ona whole and well and strong might chase the remnants of Runnos from her own mind.

"And it didn't hurt that Dante and Lucca were holed up in the wine tent by the gates," Oron said.

Avi snorted. "Special link indeed."

Oron walked into one of the amir's tents, then back out again. He held up a scroll. "I just needed to grab this. Now, let's visit Ona and see what she has been hiding under that tarp of hers."

"Tarp?" Kinneret caught up with Oron while the rest of them walked a step behind.

"Our friend Ona has a big surprise for the kyros," Oron said.

"All right. But what is that?" She pointed at the scroll.

"This is a plan I drew up for Avi's proposed new business. She asked me to do some tallying for her and double check her own findings."

Avi hadn't said a thing to Kinneret. "New business?"

"She thinks it'd be a good idea to start a library. For the Empire."

"She doesn't do anything in halves, does she?"

"With a small donation from the kyros and Amir Ekrem, she claims we could set up a delivery system for literature, philosophy, poetry, and history books between Jakobden and

Akhayma. With several stops in between for the smaller towns. I'll go over these tallies with you between archery contests today."

"As you wish."

The tents gave way to an open area at the eastern expanse of the city walls. A massive tarp covered a swathe of the striped stone. A rope lashed to a cart pulled one corner up.

Ona stood on a ladder, hair in two knots and a large paintbrush in one hand.

She turned, saw them, and waved. That was the first time she'd seen a true smile on the woman. Green paint decorated her cheek. She opened her arms to address a crowd that was quickly growing.

"Welcome visitors and friends! Please pay respect to our kyros, Seren, Pearl of the Desert!"

A striking woman in deep purple walked out of the city gates. A crown with little peaks that glittered like flames graced her brow. Kinneret squinted in the desert sun. They weren't actually flames, were they? No, they had to be gemstones. But the effect was dazzling.

The crowd erupted into cheers for the kyros. Children sat on fathers' shoulders. Warriors waved their yatagans in the air, making the sun leap from blade to blade. It was blindingly beautiful.

Lucca was positively glowing beside Dante. The look on Lucca's face answered Kinneret's unspoken question. Yes, Lucca and Seren were definitely still together.

As Calev took Oron's spot beside Kinneret—Oron was chatting with a pretty woman in blue—Seren greeted the crowd fluently in three languages.

"Welcome to the heart of the Empire. During this Gathering, we are all friends, despite any differences. Let us share our cultures, our foods, our jokes, our dances. Remember, the most beautiful weaving boasts the most varied colors. Together, you are the loveliest tapestry my eyes could ever behold."

The people shouted for her again and she silenced them by raising both hands.

"I hear that a friend of mine, Onaratta, has a surprise for me. She asked permission to do something to our walls and I'm as excited as you to see what she has done."

Ona moved the ladder away, then faced Seren. "I dedicate this work to you, Kyros Seren, for your bravery, your friendship, and your mercy." Ona looked up and waved her arms.

Five men and women at the top of the walls worked the ropes. The tarp slid to the ground with a great *whoosh*. When the plumes of sandy earth cleared, an image like Kinneret had only seen in illuminated manuscripts or fine Silvanian chapels bloomed from Akhayma's walls.

Framed in scrolling silver paint, a mosaic-style painting showed rock doves and market stalls bursting with fruit, children playing by a fountain and warriors training on the field. The shapes linked like puzzle pieces, each one leading into the other like a trick to the eye. Roses and those trees that only grew around this city branched wide and reached into a starry sky under which countless flames flickered.

Seren covered her mouth and said something in a language Kinneret didn't know. Then the kyros ran to Ona and hugged her tightly while the people cheered and shouted compliments to the creator of the mural.

"She is truly the artist she wished to be." Avi linked her arm in Kinneret's and gave Calev a smile.

Kinneret kissed Avi's temple, a contented peace flowing through her like a gentle current.

The kyros suddenly locked gazes with Kinneret. "Please join me in thanking the rest of the group who fought the forest god, Runnos, and saved our land!" Seren called out. "Thanks to you, Calev ben Y'hoshua of Old Farm, Oron the Great Sailor of the Broken Coast, Dante the brother to my love and savior of the sword Carver, and of course, the legendary Kaptan Kinneret Raza!"

The entire Gathering roared in applause and Avi leaned toward Kinneret's ear.

"I knew you were destined for great things, sister," Avi said, "but this is a little much."

"Says the girl planning to open an Empire-sized library system."

Seren took a gorgeous, wooden bow from a man and held it high. "Now it is time for me to beat you all in an archery contest!" She laughed with the crowd.

Avi elbowed Kinneret. "I'm sure you have even more plans than I do up your sleeve."

"Oh yes." Kinneret set her head on Calev's shoulder. "Just wait until Calev dazzles everyone with his dancing tonight. While they're busy staring at his handsome face, I fully plan to nab that crown off Seren's pretty head. It would look great on me and I'm certain Seren has ten others just like it." She winked, joking.

Avi slapped her. "Behave."

Kinneret grinned. "Never."

Want a complimentary prequel to this series or Alisha Klapheke's Edinburgh Seer trilogy? Go to www.alishaklapheke.com/free-prequel-1 today!

Keep reading for a sample chapter of *The Edinburgh Seer*. Magic, ancient prophecies, and romance combine in an alternate Scotland to create an adventure you'll never forget.

THE EDINBURGH SEER CHAPTER ONE SAMPLE

Summer, 2017, Fifteenth Year of John III's Reign

The morning sun had just managed to paint a pale yellow light over Edinburgh's Old Town, and, as usual, Aini MacGregor had already run three errands and set up her father's candy lab for the day's work. Pots, scrubbed and warmed, on the stove. Measuring spoons shined to make the morning sun jealous. Bags of powdered sugar and vials of hormones and chemicals standing in place like disciplined kingsmen. Everything was exactly where it needed to be.

The tower was chilly this time of day and goosebumps hurried over Aini's skin as she unscrewed a jar and shifted the newly purchased cinnamon into its tidy home. She inhaled the lovely scent. Tears burned her eyes—not because of the many spices she had at her fingertips, but because of the rasping voice carried on the wind through the cracked, leaded window above her head—the voice of Nathair Campbell, the very powerful man who would shoot her dead if he knew what she was.

A sixth-senser.

Demanding her skittering heart to quit distracting her, Aini continued about her work. Today would be a great one for her father, Lewis MacGregor, crafter of the nobility's beloved sweets. Together, with the apprentices' help, they shaped goodies that not only tasted divine, but gave the eater certain short-term abilities usually enjoyed by birds or insects, or only dreamed up by wild imaginations. They'd been a hit at the king's last birthday party. The British king was a terrible man— Aini couldn't change that—but at least his parties helped with business. With the vision-inducing gum they were about to craft and test, the MacGregor business, Enliven, was poised to rule the boutique sweets market. If only the stupid thugs, the Campbells, would leave well enough alone.

Clan Campbell worked for the king, maintaining his rules here in Scotland. But lately…they seemed to have become very full of themselves and were taking on projects that Aini was certain the king himself knew nothing about.

"Who is shouting to wake the dead in the Grassmarket?" Neve demanded in place of a *Good Morning*. Father's female apprentice padded into the room. When she wasn't working in the lab, Neve took tourists around Scotland with Caledonia Tours. She knew her history, that was for sure.

With quick fingers and a smile, the Edinburgh native pulled her hair into two high buns and secured them with pins. All the girls here wore their hair like that. Aini tugged at one of her own heavy, black locks. It refused to be tied up, but even though it made her stand out—not many half Balinese girls in Scotland—she couldn't hate it. It reminded her of her mom, a woman who hadn't been perfect, but who'd loved her completely.

Aini straightened her lab coat and eyed the king's rules hanging on the wall. An identical list of "Scottish citizens cannot do this" and "All citizens and colonials must do that" were posted in every pub, home, and store in the entire British Empire. Even across the pond in the rebellious Dominion of New England colonies. Aini wondered if they'd ever get over their 18th century loss. They were nearly as bad as the Scottish rebels here.

Blinking, she remembered Neve's earlier question. "Nathair Campbell is down there, dirtying the morning."

Neve made a Scottish sound of disgust in the back of her throat. Aini couldn't have agreed more. "I'm excited about that new gum recipe," Neve said.

Perfectly on time—because Aini perfectly timed it—the gum base started to bubble on the stove.

"Your white pepper idea for the gum is going to work. I can feel it." Aini wiped her hands on a towel, breathing in the sweet smells. "I really think it'll trigger the chewer's schema for fire."

Neve grinned, and Aini realized her Dominion of New England accent was blazing again.

Thane loped into the lab, and Aini's heart whirred like a broken taffy puller and pushed every other thought out of her head. At six-foot-four, the Scotsman dominated the room, all broad shoulders, gray flashing eyes, and downturned mouth. He pulled his glasses out of his messy, honey-colored hair and headed toward his lab coat on the far hook. Mud caked the toes of his boots, and a silver necklace winked from his collarbone.

Because of who Aini was, and *what* Aini was, Thane with his late nights and penchant for whisky was the very definition of

Look, but don't touch. She had to be careful. Do nothing dangerous. Never break any rules.

"Good morning, Thane."

Just because he wasn't for her didn't mean she had to be rude. After all, he was Father's favorite, besides herself, of course. Thane had developed the original formula for the vision gum. Aini wished she had half the brains he did.

"We're almost ready to mix," she said.

His gaze slid over her fingers and up her arms, and he gave her a nod.

As Neve measured out the pepper, Aini held a hand toward the bubbling broiler. "A little help?" she asked Thane. Her face heated. Why did her cheeks have to flush so easily?

"Aye. Course." Thane's thick, West Scots accent wrapped around every O and tripped over each R beautifully.

Tugging his coat on, Thane slid his glasses onto his slightly overlarge nose. Tattoos of chemical formulas snaked down his fingers in black letters, tiny numbers, and mathematical symbols. Aini leaned forward a little. NaCl was salt. Another finger had a *V* over a *t* and—*oh*—it was the formula for viscosity. But the other markings? She could never quite get a good look at them.

Father walked in, wearing his usual style—all black under his lab coat, and every item ironed into full submission. He winked before readying the powdered sugar at the lab's silver table. He still wore his wedding ring, though the divorce happened long before Aini's mother died two years ago. She sighed, wishing she could do something about that pain.

"I was thinking," Father said to Thane, "if we used a pressure cooker to force the Maillard reaction in tomorrow's Dulce de Leche recipe..."

Thane's face brightened. "We could decrease the cooking time by perhaps six times." Thane lifted the pot as Aini stirred. His arm brushed hers and she swallowed. "Genius, Mr. MacGregor," Thane said.

"Will you never stop with the Mr. MacGregor? Just Lewis, please."

Thane smiled at Father like he was his own, like Father could somehow heal the hurt that clouded the uni student's eyes. But it was all right. She wasn't jealous. Aini knew Father was good at providing a stable life, a simple and scheduled way of living, something maybe Thane hadn't experienced before apprenticing here.

"Neve, will you please warm up the mixer?" Father wiped a spot of sugar off his nose and set his planner on the desk near the far end of the lab. The green and blue sugar, in the jars he'd mounted on the whitewashed wall, sparkled. He frowned like there was something unpleasant about them. Aini touched her chin. She'd always wondered why he displayed the jars like that. They'd never used those colored sugars and surely it would be better to have them with the other ingredients, organized by the lab table. She'd look into it later.

Father shook his head and went to help Thane pour the steaming gum base into the powdered sugar.

The lab's landline rang and Aini picked up. A familiar, rough voice asked for Lewis MacGregor. Aini gritted her teeth. Not *them* again. Her grip on the phone tightened.

"Hold please." She looked to Father. "It's for you."

He stared at the ceiling, eyes pressed closed, before finally taking the call.

While Neve dealt with the mixer's perpetually moody switch across the room—all while humming a song loved by

Father's other male apprentice, Myles—Aini took Father's place beside Thane.

Plunging her hands into the gum blend, she kneaded the sticky stuff. The mix was ready for flavor. The powdered sage, white pepper, and smoky nutmeg did nothing to improve the color of the chewing gum, but she was pretty sure Neve was on to something with this flavor choice. The herbs and spices, along with the medieval art packaging that Myles had drawn up, might just get people seeing ancient castles and feasts in great halls. Chemistry crossed with suggestion. It was how the human brain worked.

"No." Father's knuckles whitened as he squeezed the phone. "I'm not going to weaponize my products. Not until I see the royal approval. I'm finished talking about this." He punched a button and threw the phone to his desk where it banged against his laptop. "Campbells. Pushing and pushing. Playing both sides, and I know very well I'm not going to be the winner no matter how..." Muttering, he stalked back to the table. "I need to get something from my downstairs office. Give me a shout when we're ready to test." He disappeared down the staircase, growling about being left in peace.

The Campbells made up the majority of kingsmen stationed in Edinburgh. Normally, they were the law, acting as the king's agents, along with the other kingsmen. But since that public execution of those rebels last month, things had been different. Nathair Campbell had executed Scottish subjects without a trial of any kind. The king had excused him, blaming overzealous loyalty to the crown, but Aini wasn't so sure. Clan Campbell was less an arm of the king and more of a criminal gang these days. Aini couldn't believe they were pressuring Father to develop products that could covertly paralyze and poison without the king's seal of approval. Even if it was to fight the rebels. It was unfathomable.

Thane breathed hard through his nose like an angry horse.

She eyed the gum, looking for dry spots or uneven spicing. "What is it? What's off?"

Vine-like muscles twisted below Thane's rolled coat sleeves. He dusted his hands off and pushed his glasses into his hair. "If your father would agree to aid the Campbells, he'd be helping Scotland fight the rebels."

"He doesn't want to twist our craft into something sick and evil." She put her hands on her hips and powdered sugar puffed like little clouds. Flushing, she brushed herself off. "He's worked long and hard to establish Enliven. It's a boutique candy supplier. Not a government laboratory. Besides that, why can't the Campbells go through the official channels and find their own chemists if they're so set on this?"

Neve gathered the pre-blended gum mix. "Because Mr. MacGregor is the best chemist in the empire and they know it."

"Well, we're going to follow the official rules." Aini crossed her arms. "The king could shut us down and you know it."

Neve opened her mouth and closed it again. She hurried to the mixer and dropped her bundle into the metal bowl.

Aini chewed the inside of her cheek. She didn't want to be hard on Neve, but the rules were the rules.

"The Campbells and the king have the same goal, don't they?" Thane frowned. "What difference does fussing about with royal seals make?"

"If my father skirts the law like the Campbells want him to do, the Campbells might get away with it, but I seriously doubt he will."

An image flashed through her memory—an executed sixth-senser.

The woman had been about her mother's age. Aini remembered the lady's wispy, auburn hair. The black band across her eyes. Her body jerking as the bullet hit her chest. The red blood against her striped dress. Her clothing said native Edinburgh, the style Aini tried to imitate. But even fitting in hadn't saved her.

If Aini was found out, the Campbells would assume Father knew about her ability, which he didn't. She squeezed her hands together. She couldn't even think about him rotting in a dark cell.

When the gum was mixed and cooled, Thane cut the ropes into small pieces and Aini called her father back up to the lab. It was time to see if the gum really worked.

The light through the lab's windows cast a net of gold around Aini's father as he peered at his watch. He handed Aini the clipboard of notes they'd destroy as soon as the trial was complete. They couldn't let anyone outside of Enliven get a hold of the information. The competition would leap at the chance to outdo them. Because of this, Aini and the rest had become very, very good at remembering recipes.

Neve and Aini found seats and Thane took a stool, ready to try the gum.

"Where is Myles anyway?" Neve asked.

Aini was actually glad Father's second male apprentice wasn't here. "Buying new paints for his adverts." Myles was great fun, but he could really be a distraction during tests like this.

Father stared at Thane. "I want to know the very minute—

the exact moment—you see something." He started the timer on his watch.

"Aye," Thane popped the gum between his lips and chewed, rubbing a hand over his sharp chin.

"How's it taste, then?" Neve scooted forward on her stool.

"A bit fiery."

"Fiery?" Aini asked, pen poised over the clipboard. "Be more specific. We need details for the investors."

"Any visions yet?" Father inched closer to Thane.

Stumbling back, Thane's mouth dropped open, the gum on his tongue.

Aini laughed.

Father practically hopped on Thane. "What do you see, lad?" He normally hid his accent, wanting to please his many English clients, but excitement drew it right out of him.

Staring at the ceiling beams, Thane paled. "Translucent wings. About ten feet long. He's...he's..." The uni student ducked and laughed once, his Adam's apple bobbing in his throat. "He's breathing fire." He shoved his hands through his hair and knocked his glasses to the floor.

Neve hugged herself. "A dragon."

Father lifted his feet in a little jig and grabbed Aini's arm, pulling her into his dance. Heart light, she did a spin, then squeezed him, feeling safe and loved, as if everything was going to be okay.

"I can't believe it," Thane whispered.

Neve grinned. "I knew that white pepper would do the trick."

"Couldn't have done it without you, my wee squirrel," Father said to Aini. "The king will reward us handsomely, what with his birthday celebration coming up. We might get a tax exemption."

"And the elite will want it at their parties if the king has it at his," she said.

Father shouted, "Huzzah!" and zipped over to his desk to write something up.

Aini couldn't stop smiling. Another candy for their impressive inventory. Another building block for Father's beloved business. Somehow, she had to thank the apprentices for all their hard work. Maybe a special dinner or a big night out. This vision-inducing gum was another reason she loved having all of them here, a part of the family.

Neve peppered Thane with questions about the formula. Over Neve's head, Thane met Aini's gaze. A shadow passed over his face. He was a melancholy sort, but this was more. Something…darker. Aini's smile faded. He had nothing to be upset about today. What could be bothering him? Surely not all this stuff about the Campbells. It would pass. Wouldn't it?

Father tugged Aini into another jubilant hug, and her smile returned. She could maintain this happiness. She would maintain it. No matter what. She just had to keep her sixth sense concealed. Because visions prompted by chewing gum earned money, but visions of another sort only led to death.

Grab the complete trilogy today!
https://www.amazon.com/dp/B07BP1ZNPR

www.ingramcontent.com/pod-product-compliance
Lightning Source LLC
Chambersburg PA
CBHW021010120726
47905CB00009B/2943